Serving Sarah

An erotic novel

by Molly Sands

'To my own sweet Severin with love and laughter.'

Also by Molly Sands – Cruel Heaven, The Devlin Woman, A New Devotion, An Obedient Husband, Magda, Slave Song, Contessa, Sacred Days.

'Be then my slave, and know what it means to be delivered into the hands of a woman.' (Leopold von Sacher-Masoch, 'Venus in Furs.')

SERVING SARAH

'Why don't you call me by that other name?' Sarah whispered. 'I won't mind if you do.'

'What's the matter, Charles?' Sarah asked her husband, surprised to find him home from work before her. His tie undone, and looking very cast-down, he was slumped at the breakfast bar drinking whisky.

'I didn't get it,' he said, not looking at her.

The 'it' in question was the post of CEO at Joseph & Hill Investment. He'd been doing the job in a stand-in capacity for over a year while Simon Stevas, the existing CEO, recovered from a heart condition, but illness had finally forced Simon to retire, and the board had invited Charles to apply for the post. Under Charles' interim leadership the company had thrived, morale was high, and he'd expected the interview to be a formality.

'The bastards,' said Sarah, strangely thrilled to hear of her husband's failure. 'Who did they give it to?'

'Ryan Moore,' said Charles.

Sarah knew that would hurt Charles. He'd appointed Ryan as his depute six months ago. Ryan was twelve years younger than Charles, but they'd become friends, playing golf and going to football games together. Yet Sarah wasn't surprised by Ryan's success. She'd met him a few times at staff parties and found him good-looking and charming, but she'd seen the hard gleam of ambition in his eyes. Like Charles, he kept it well hidden, but it was there.

'I didn't know he was going for it,' said Sarah.

'Neither did I,' said Charles. 'He never said a word. He even went over my interview with me, the bastard. He knew what I was going to say, and he'll have used that to undermine me in his presentation.'

'Now that was dirty,' said Sarah, once more strangely thrilled.

'And I thought we were friends,' said Charles. 'What a bloody fool I've been.'

'Have you spoken to him since?'

'Oh, we shook hands and did the all's fair in love and war routine, but we can never be friends again. That's dead and buried, believe me. He even asked me to stay on and work under him,' said Charles, pouring himself another whisky. 'Can you imagine?'

'What did you say?' Sarah asked, intrigued by the idea of Charles working under someone.

'What do you think I said? I refused point blank.'

'You didn't resign, did you?'

'Of course not, but I've indicated to the board I'll consider a package. I'll hear in a few days, I'm sure. They'll want it sorted quickly.'

'Will you be going in meantime?'

'I have some weeks due. I'll take those, and stay at home and look for a new job. I won't take this lying down.'

'I'm sure you won't,' said Sarah who knew how competitive Charles became when roused. 'All I can say is that it's their loss, and you'll get another job in no time. You're far too good at what you do to be idle for long.'

She gave him a hug and a kiss, and he hugged her back, saying, 'Thank-you, Sarah, that means a lot, you've no idea.'

Hearing the tenderness in his voice, she felt a fondness for him that reassured her. This is more like it, she thought. This is how a wife is supposed to feel about her husband.

'No matter what happens,' she said, 'you've always got me.'

'I know,' he said.

'I want you to remember that.'

'I will.'

'For better or for worse.'

'I love you,' he said.

'I'll cook something nice for dinner,' she said, giving him another hug, 'and then we'll relax and take it easy. I don't want you to worry.'

'I won't,' he said, very glad of his loyal and loving wife.

Yet, as she prepared their meal, Sarah's thoughts weren't entirely loyal. Charles had led a charmed life – inheriting money and a lovely town-house from his parents, now deceased, and enjoying a successful and well-paid career – and so he wasn't used to not getting his own way. As his wife, Sarah had benefited from his good fortune, and yet she took pleasure in his set-back at work. She knew she wasn't being fair. Coming from a poor background, marrying Charles had brought her security and comfort as well as two lovely daughters who were both thriving in the early stages of their careers, Kate as a schoolteacher in York, and Emily as a speech therapist in Edinburgh. What's more, Charles had always been faithful and kind, as well as supportive of her in her own career as an accountant specialising in overseas trade. And he was a good-looking man – a model husband in so many ways. 'You are being unfair,' Sarah scolded herself. Charles had given her a happy and comfortable life, and she had no reason to wish him ill.

And yet her enjoyment persisted, turning to a faint yet unmistakable arousal and, later that night while they were undressing for bed, she found herself hoping Charles would want to play out his fantasy. In all their years of marriage she'd acted it for him only a handful of times, always after something had gone wrong in his life, and after he'd been drinking, but those few occasions had made a strong impression on her, alerted her to a very different side to her husband, and possibly, to herself.

It was a scenario that seemed to bring Charles refuge from anxiety and stress, and tonight the stars were definitely aligned, but she knew how ashamed he was of his desires. She'd tried to talk to him about them a number of times – she was curious about his fantasies and open to exploring them – but each time he'd pretended he had no idea what she was talking about, and months, sometimes years would go by before his needs once more grew too strong to be suppressed.

Sarah understood how hard it must be for him to accept his desires. As a successful man accustomed to power and influence, he would judge them, she had no doubt, to be weak and unmanly, a frailty in his character that shouldn't be encouraged or tolerated under any circumstances, and so she decided to help things along a little. She'd been drinking too, and it was fun to cast aside her 'good wife' persona, and besides, it was a wife's duty to help her husband in his time of need. Sometimes in life bad was good she told herself.

'Shall I keep my slip on in bed?' she asked him casually as she stepped out of her skirt.

'Hm?' Charles said as if he hadn't heard, but Sarah had seen his shoulders stiffen, and his cheeks redden with embarrassment.

'It was nothing,' she said. 'Silly of me, really. I was just wondering if you'd like me to wear my slip to bed, that's all.'

She knew he had a thing about slips – he'd often buy her a new one for Christmas or for her birthday, a neatly wrapped little package handed to her with a shy look – and she was wearing a particularly elegant one with thin shoulder straps and a pretty lace hem that made her feel desirable and aloof, the femme fatale in an Italian film, she imagined, thinking of the lovely Monica Vitti in Michelangelo Antonioni's hauntingly erotic 'L'Avventura,' one of her favourite films.

'I'll keep my tights and panties on too if you like,' she said.

'Only if you want to,' he said, blushing heavily and not looking at her.

'Oh, well,' she said, 'I won't bother then.'

'No,' he said quickly. 'Keep them on, you may as well.'

Got you.

'They're quite pretty knickers,' she said, lifting her slip to let him see. 'Don't you think?'

He raised his head and looked at her, taken aback by her unusually bold display, and finding the glimpse of her panties beneath her sheer hose utterly beguiling.

'And these are my favourite tights,' she said, running a hand down her thigh. She had naturally good legs, and wasn't averse to showing them off. 'They're beautifully soft and smooth, you'll love them, I'm sure.'

'They're very nice,' he said, wishing his voice had been steadier.

'Poor Charles,' she said, coming round to his side of the bed where he was standing in his boxer shorts holding his pyjamas. 'You've had a hard and upsetting day, and I know you like me in a slip. I just want to help if I can, make you feel better.'

Putting her arms around him, she kissed him deeply, pleased to feel he was erect.

'There,' she said, pressing against him. 'That's better now, isn't it?'

'Yes,' he said meekly, moved by her kindness.

'Shall I keep my slip on?'

'Yes,' he said.

'Say please, then,' she said, taking a risk.

'Please,' he said, his voice heavy with desire.

'Alright, then, I will,' she said.

She was pleased she'd got him to open up. Now she could take things further.

'If I'm going to keep my slip on,' she said, taking his pyjamas from him and dropping them on the floor, 'you won't need these silly things, will you?'

'No,' he said, very aroused. The events of the day had left him weak and defeated, alcohol had loosened his inhibitions, and Sarah seemed to know exactly what he wanted. It was a shameful thing for a man to want, and he knew he should fight it, but he was tired of fighting, and Sarah was so loving, and so beautiful in her silky slip and with that smile on her face, that he knew he could hide no longer.

'And you won't need these either,' she said, tugging down his boxer shorts and pushing her hips, so warm beneath her slip, against his naked erection. Touching her legs against his to let him feel how smooth her nylons were, she kissed him again, and then pulled him down with her into bed, lying on her side, and holding him close. 'Here,' she whispered, guiding his head between her lace-covered breasts, 'it's what you want, what you need.'

Giving a long sigh, he kissed her erect nipples through her slip, loving her scented warmth.

'This is for you, Charles,' she said, holding him tight. 'It's all for you.'

'God, Sarah, I love you.'

'I should think you do,' she said to tease him, 'but there's another name you like to call me if I'm not mistaken. It's not always plain old Sarah, is it? Sometimes you like me to be someone else.'

She felt him tense, but wine had emboldened her, and she was damned is she was going to back down. He could hide if he wanted, but that didn't mean she had to.

'Why don't you call me by that other name?' Sarah whispered. 'I won't mind if you do. I might even like it.'

A tremor passed through him, and he kept his face hidden between her breasts.

'Oh, come on Charles, you must remember,' she coaxed him, a smile in her voice. 'At Christmas, when we got home from Marion's party. You were drunk, and upset after arguing with Anthony about politics. You told him the Tories were a bunch of self-regarding grifters. But you didn't call me Sarah that night did you?' she said, trapping his erection beneath her warm, nylon-clad thigh. 'Oh no, you called me by a very different name that night, you must remember.'

'I don't,' he lied.

'Well, I do,' she said. 'It made quite an impression on me, believe me. Such an impression I've never forgotten it.'

'I don't remember,' he said again, anxiety making him light-headed.

'Oh, I'm sure you do, Charles,' she said. 'You're just too scared to admit it.'

'Oh, God,' he said, his head still between her breasts.

'You don't have to be scared,' she whispered, stroking his hair. 'I'm your wife, I won't hurt you, you know that, don't you?'

He said nothing, just gave a timid nod.

'You're in the safest place in the world.'

He gave another nod, nuzzling against the lace of her slip.

'Well, then,' she said softly, weaving her spell, 'you can call me whatever you like. Where's the harm if it lets you escape for a while? It's only a little fun between man and wife, and everyone deserves a little fun, don't you think? So, come on now, be a brave boy and tell me what you called me after Marion's party.'

He muttered something so quietly she couldn't make out what he'd said.

'Honestly, Charles,' she said, laughing warmly in a way she hoped might reassure him, 'you sound like a little mouse. You can do much better than that, a big, important man like you. Speak up, and let me hear you.'

'M-mistress,' he stammered loud enough for her to hear.

'There, it's said,' she said, holding him tight, and feeling a sweet spasm of arousal. 'That wasn't so bad, was it?'

'N-no.'

'I beg your pardon,' she said, making her voice stern.

'No, Mistress,' he said timidly.

'More like it,' she said, taking down a strap of her slip and leading his mouth to her uncovered breast. 'And here's your reward for being a good boy, for having the courage to tell the truth.' He groaned and suckled eagerly, and she moved her thigh and put her hand on his cock, pleased to find he was fiercely erect.

'Someone likes calling me Mistress,' she said, cupping his balls and running her fingers up and down his length. 'Someone likes it very much.'

He groaned, and pushed against her hand.

'That's lovely,' she said. 'All hard for your Mistress, all hard and ready.'

Still caressing him, she shifted a little, giving him her other breast, and whispering softly, 'You don't have to worry any more, Charles. You don't have to be the big, strong man, not here, not with me. You can be anything you like, you can be my sweet little boy for as long as you like. You can be my slave.'

She felt him tense and try to pull away, but she held him tight in her strong, slim arms.

'What's wrong?' she said, 'don't you like being called a slave? It's only a word, and you don't have to be frightened of a word, do you? Of course not, and if you call me Mistress it's only right I call you slave. You can't have one without the other, can you?'

His mouth at her breast, he made a strange muffled sound, and she asked him again, 'Can you, Charles?'

'N-no,' he stammered.

'That's right,' she said. 'It's an equation. If I'm your Mistress you must be my slave, isn't that correct?'

'Yes.'

'Yes, who?'

'Yes, Mistress.'

'So what are you?'

Too ashamed to say it, he made a groaning sound instead.

'Say it, Charles,' she insisted. 'I want to hear you say it.'

'Your slave,' he confessed, another tremor passing through him.

'That's right, you are,' she said approvingly, giving him her breast again, aroused by the way he latched on like an infant. 'And now you're my slave, I can tell you what to do, can't I?'

'Mmf,' he groaned, kissing her breast.

'I can give you instructions?'

'Yes,' he said, a tremble in his voice.

'Issue commands to my heart's content?'

'Y-yes.'

'In fact, I can do whatever I like with you.'

'Yes.'

'What fun,' she said through laughter. 'And you'll have to obey me, won't you?'

'Yes.'

'No matter what?'

'Yes.'

'A slave has to obey his Mistress,' she declared, a mockery in her voice that sharpened his arousal. 'It's the only point of his existence, his sole purpose – to see to her comfort and pleasure, to earn her praise and good opinion. To suffer for her if he has to. To dedicate his life to her happiness, isn't that right, Charles?'

'Yes, Mistress.'

'He has no choice in the matter, does he?' she said, both aroused and amused by her play-acting, and by the depth of his submission.

'No.'

'None at all.'

'None,' he agreed, his head spinning.

'Come on, then,' she said, tugging down her panties and hose. 'You know what your Mistress likes, you know what she wants from her slave.'

His mouth was already moving down her stomach to her slick cunt where he worshipped with a passion that delighted Sarah. In their everyday marriage Charles seldom pleasured her in this way, but as her slave he seemed to long to perform it for her, and she welcomed his devotion as a rare sensual treat. Her pleasure mounting quickly, she pulled his mouth against her, taking control of him in a way that thrilled her.

'That's it,' she said, her voice husky now. 'Love your Mistress, love her the way a slave should.'

Charles may have been a novice at this kind of sex, but his passion, born from the joy he found in submission, more than made up for his lack of experience, and Sarah gripped his hair and tugged it violently as her pleasure grew urgent.

'I can do what I like with you,' she moaned, barely aware of what she was saying. 'Anything I fucking well like … I own you … I rule you … With my voice, with my clothes, with my legs, with my cunt … I fucking own you …'

Normally very proper, it aroused Sarah greatly to use such language, language she considered 'dirty,' and she gloried in her freedom to do and speak as she liked.

Also aroused by her profanity, and by how much it seemed to excite Sarah to take control of him, Charles worshipped harder and deeper so that Sarah threw back her head, and arched her back in joy.

'Oh, God,' she cried out as she came. 'Oh God, oh God.'

Her joy woke a deeper hunger in Charles, and he moved upwards, kissing her stomach, her breasts, and then her lips as he pushed his erection inside her, thrusting with a vigour that made the bed shake. To her delight Sarah felt another wave of pleasure rise within her. Charles was lost in a fever of desire, she could taste herself on his lips, and nothing mattered except their savage joy in each other. God, she loved this. Always so polite and steady in her daily life, it felt wonderful to be wanton and selfish, a woman free to enjoy her sexual power, a Mistress strong enough to enslave the man in her life, bind him eternally to her service.

'Is that the best you can do?' she gasped, wanting to taunt him, keep him in his place. 'I expect better from a slave … Much better.'

She laughed when he thrust harder and deeper, and then matched his rhythm, digging her nails into his back, and hissing, 'Show me how a slave serves his Mistress … Show me how he loves her …'

Gripping the cold iron bars of the bedstead, Charles pounded into her, striving to please his Mistress. 'I love you,' he cried out as if in pain. 'I love you, I love you …'

'Then come for me,' she commanded. 'Come for your Mistress … Come now … I want it all … Everything … Give it to me now.'

Crying out like an animal, he obeyed her, surrendering to a pleasure so strong it left him dazed and barely conscious. Sarah had plunged over the cliff with him, exulting in his passion for her, a passion provoked by her power over him, by her woman's strength and authority.

Stunned by pleasure, they exchanged dreamy endearments, but only one thought rose to the surface of Sarah's mind as they drifted into sleep – that she'd loved being his Mistress, and she wanted more. Much more.

BUT IF Sarah thought it was going to be easy to get what she wanted she quickly discovered she was mistaken. For the next two days Charles was moody and evasive, keeping to his study and not even joining her for meals. She'd expected him to retreat into himself – it was what he'd always done in the past after surrendering to her – but she hadn't expected him to be so short-tempered, or so miserable. And on top of that, the house was a mess. Jenny, their cleaner of many years, had recently moved back to Cornwall to be with her daughter who'd given birth to twins, and they hadn't found a replacement. Sarah was exceptionally busy at work, and she resented coming home to a messy house.

'If you can't be cheerful,' she told him sharply on Thursday morning, 'you can at least be useful around the house,' but he made no reply, just poured himself more coffee. Her anger rising, she refused to let him off the hook. 'I've had enough of you moping around like this. When I get back tonight I expect to come home to a clean house. I'll expect the whole house to be vacuumed, the washing done, and a start made on the ironing. And you can do a supermarket shopping and pick up my dry-cleaning,' she said, taking the dry-cleaners' stub from her purse, and putting it down on the table. 'Have you heard me?'

When he didn't reply, she slammed her hand on the table, making him jump.

'I asked you a question, Charles, and you'll have the good manners to answer it.'

'I heard you,' he said, as truculent as a teenager.

'I very much hope you have,' she said, a steely glint in her eyes. 'I'm not putting up with this, so there's something else that's going to happen. We're going to have a talk tonight whether you want one or not. We're going to talk about work and money and the way you've been behaving. And we'll talk about sex too. And don't give me that look. We're not living in the nineteenth century, and we've been married for over twenty years, surely to God we can have a conversation about sex. I mean it, Charles,' she said, taking up her coat and bag, and calling to him on her way through the hall, 'so you'd better be ready.'

She slammed the front-door on the way out and felt the better for it, but she had a trying and difficult day at work, and she felt anxious on her way home, worried about what she might find, so she was relieved to find the house tidy, and Charles in a contrite and more approachable frame of mind.

'You've been busy,' she said, looking round the clean kitchen as he handed her a glass of wine.

'I've been at it all day,' he said. 'I've vacuumed and done the ironing, and put away the shopping. I've even cleaned the bathroom.'

'Did you pick up my dry-cleaning?' She had a meeting in the morning with one of her biggest clients, and she wanted to wear her smartest suit.

'It's hanging up in your wardrobe.'

'Gold star,' she said.

'Only one?' said Charles, pleased with himself.

'And something smells nice.'

'I've made the casserole you like.'

'Thank-you, Charles,' she said, kissing him on the cheek. 'I really appreciate this – coming home to a clean house and a friendly husband. It makes all the difference.'

'It's the least you deserve,' he said, a sheepish look on his face. 'I've been impossible. I'm sorry, and I hope you'll forgive me.'

'Of course I forgive you,' she said, 'but only if you hurry up and feed me.'

After their meal they sat with their wine on the couch in the sitting-room, and had the talk Sarah had promised.

'So it's all done and dusted?' Sarah said, surprised to hear that Charles had already agreed a severance package from work.

'It's actually better than I'd hoped,' said Charles. 'They wanted rid of me as quickly as possible, and they were willing to pay for it. Guilt money as much as anything else.'

'That's good news,' said Sarah, going on to remind him of their good fortune. 'We're so lucky, Charles. You inherited this lovely house along with money from your parents, I have work, we have savings and excellent pensions, and our children are happy and well, thank God. We're not rich, but we're very well-off. It wouldn't matter if you never worked again. Think how many people would love to be in that position, so you mustn't be down about work. Try and put it in perspective, and move on. When I think of all the terrible things we see every time we watch the news, all those people in the world with no homes, no money, no food – my God, we live like kings – and yet we're never happy, always wanting more. It's time you gave thanks for all you've got instead of being angry about what you've lost.'

'I know,' he said, 'but I can't stand the way that bastard got the better of me.'

'Who says he did?' said Sarah. 'Ryan's got all the pressure and anxiety of running a company while you can take a break, do what you like for a while. It sounds to me like you got the better of him.'

'If you say so, but that's not how it feels. I can't even bear the sound of his name.'

'Only because of your conditioning,' said Sarah. 'Only because of your male pride. Let that go and everything will look very different.'

'It's not just pride,' said Charles. 'I liked him. I thought he was my friend, really I did.'

'Well, if he was, he wasn't a friend worth having. You're well shot of him.'

'I'd like to punch him.'

'Not a good idea.'

'Why not?'

'He's younger and bigger than you.'

'I don't care, it would be worth it.'

'Forget him,' said Sarah. 'That's better than any punch.'

'Is it?'

'Much,' she said. 'It shows you don't care.'

'But I do care,' he said. 'And I hate to lose.'

'At work, maybe,' she said, a gleam in her eye, 'but not in bed.'

'What's that supposed to mean?' he said, surprised by her sudden change of tack.

'You didn't mind losing the other night,' she said, a teasing edge to her voice that infuriated and aroused him. 'Not when I was your Mistress and you were my slave. In fact, I seem to remember you rather liked it.'

'I don't want to talk about this,' Charles said, going to get up from the couch.

'Stay where you are,' Sarah said firmly, holding him back by an arm. 'I told you this morning we were going to do this, and I meant it.'

'And I told you I don't want to talk about it,' he said with a hard finality he was sure would end the matter.

'Well, I do want to talk about it,' Sarah replied, showing no sign of backing down, 'or does what I want not count for anything? Is everything in this house only about the great Charles Hunter?'

He looked at her with murder in his eyes, but she wouldn't be put off.

'This isn't just about you,' she told him, matching his fierce gaze, 'and we've been tiptoeing around this for years. It's high time you stopped hiding, and talked to me about what you like.'

'No,' he said, not looking at her.

'What do you mean, no?' she said, her temper rising.

'What does no always mean?' he said coldly.

'You're hiding again,' she said, her heart pounding, 'and I won't take no for an answer, I mean it, Charles, not this time.'

'It's not going to happen.'

'It most certainly is going to happen.'

'You're out of line here, Sarah.'

'I'm out of line?' she said, outraged. 'My God, what harm can talking do? It's only sex, for heaven's sake. You may be frightened of it, but I'm not. So you like to be my slave, so what? It makes you ashamed to want such a thing, so what? What's a little embarrassment after twenty-five tears of marriage? And what about me? Don't I have a say in this? I liked what we did the other night, in case you want to know. It was fun to be the one in charge, to be your Mistress, and I'm not ashamed to admit it.'

'You liked it?' he said.

'Couldn't you tell?'

'I thought … I thought … ' he mumbled, unable to order his thoughts.

'What did you think?'

'That you were pretending,' he said, pain in his eyes. 'That you were doing it for me.'

'Giving you what you want?'

'Yes.'

'Being the good little wife?'

'I suppose so.'

'Maybe I was,' she said, 'but that doesn't mean I didn't enjoy it. I liked being the one in charge. It felt different, sexy. It turned me on, and I don't see anything wrong with that.'

'Don't you?' he said, a genuine need to know in his voice.

'I really don't,' she said, sensing a chink in his armour. 'It's only sex, and I don't see why we shouldn't talk about it the way we talk about everything else.'

'I don't think I can, Sarah.'

'Why not? Don't you trust me?'

'Of course I do, but this is different.'

'In what way?'

'It just is.'

'That's not an answer.'

'I don't know how to talk about it.'

'Then, try.'

'That kind of sex, it's stupid and wrong, and I don't understand it,' he said. 'It's weak of me, and it makes me ashamed. That's all I want to say.'

'I don't see what's wrong or stupid about it, or weak for that matter, and there are lots of things in the world we don't understand,' she said, putting her hand on his, and squeezing gently. 'And of course it makes you ashamed, a big, important man like you surrendering to your wife, being her slave and calling her Mistress. Imagine such a thing,' she said, laughter in her eyes. 'It's probably the shame that makes you like it so much, the thrill of doing what you know you shouldn't. The thrill of the forbidden.'

'God knows what it is,' he said.

'You see, you can talk about it,' she said gently. 'And I think it might be good for us if you did.'

'There are some things that shouldn't be talked about.'

'I won't bite,' she said, leaning in and biting his ear, making him laugh so that, for a moment, they were newlyweds again.

'Alright, I'll try,' said Charles.

'I appreciate that, Charles, really I do.'

Very nervous and ill-at-ease, he put his head back and breathed out slowly.

'Have you always wanted it?' she asked.

'Ever since I was a boy,' he said. 'There were no girls at my boarding-school, and so girls always seemed unreachable and perfect. From then on I think I've always put women on a pedestal.'

'You've never found out we're just ordinary creatures getting through life like everyone else?'

'I don't believe I ever have,' he said. 'Of course, intellectually I know that's true, but knowledge and feelings are very different things. Women have always seemed magical to me.'

'Goddesses?'

'In a way.'

'And frightening?'

'Yes, that too.'

'Why?'

'I don't know, maybe it's because they've got what I want and I'm frightened they won't give it to me.'

'You mean sex?'

'Not just sex. Love, friendship, respect, family, children. I think most of all I'm frightened they won't respect me.'

'Why, because you want to be their slave?'

'Something like that, it's a twisted bloody thing.'

'So you want what you most fear?' she said, squeezing his hand again, and smiling warmly. 'You want to risk not being respected.'

'Maybe,' he said, returning her smile, and beginning to feel a little less anxious. 'Honestly, it's too fucked up to say anything for sure.'

'I think we're all fucked up one way or another, and everyone's got something they're hiding. Didn't the writer Marquez once say, "All human beings have three lives – public, private and secret?"'

'I've never heard that before.'

'I think he's right, though.'

'So there's nothing wrong with me, is that what you're saying? I'm just an ordinary guy?'

'I think maybe that's exactly what you are, except perhaps you have an unusually strong drive to succeed, and therefore an equally strong fear of failure.'

'Thank-you, Doctor.'

'You'll receive my bill in the post.'

'So what are you hiding, then? What's your secret?'

'I'm very dull, I'm not sure I have one.'

'Now who's the coward?'

'Alright, then,' she said. 'Maybe there's a little part of me that likes the idea of being cruel to my wealthy and handsome husband.'

'You don't have a cruel bone in your body.'

'That's what you think,' she said, feeling an elusive arousal. 'You'd better watch out, Charles, I'm warning you. Maybe I've spent all these years lulling you into a false sense of security, and soon you'll discover the real me – then you'll be sorry.'

'I can't wait,' he said, laughing, and not taking her seriously.

Greatly to his surprise, it felt good to talk about hidden things, and much easier than he'd thought possible. Sarah made it easy, but then Sarah made everything easy, and always had throughout their marriage. God, he was lucky to have her.

'Have you ever done anything about it?' Sarah asked. She knew he'd had a lot of girlfriends before they'd met, many of them rich and good-looking.

'You mean, before you?' he said.

'Certainly not after, I hope,' she said in mock outrage.

'Of course not after,' he said, suddenly on his honour.

'I was only teasing, Charles.'

For some reason Charles' school trunk, still stored in the attic after all these years with his initials C.A.W.H on it in gold lettering, came into Sarah's mind. The handsome, well-off Charles Arnold William Hunter had been quite a catch in his day.

'I've never looked at other women, not after we met, you know that perfectly well.'

'I do know it,' she said, moved by his devotion. She knew he'd always been faithful to her, just as she'd always been faithful to him.

'I've never even been tempted.'

'And I'm very glad to hear it,' she said, putting a hand gently on his arm. 'But before me?'

'That was different,' he said. 'One girl in particular.'

'One girl?' she said, intrigued.

'Yes.'

'What was so particular about her?'

'It hurts to think about it.'

'Oh, get on with it,' she said, more amused than impatient, but even more intrigued.

'I met her in my first year at Cambridge,' he said shyly. 'Caroline Webster. The first time we met she saw right through me. She just had that look – a speck of derision in the corner of her eye. I don't know how she knew – I barely knew myself – but she could tell what I wanted. Either that, or she was born that way. To this day, I don't know if she tuned in to something in me, or if it was something she wanted all along for her own reasons. I've often wondered if she treated other men the same way, or if it was just me.'

'Maybe you were the lucky one.'

'More like unlucky.'

'What did she do to you?'

'Do you really want to know?'

'Guess?' said Sarah.

'She was very clever,' Charles said, 'but she was lazy, and she decided it was a good idea to make me write her essays. She'd get dressed up and go out to clubs and parties while I stayed at home and did her work for her.'

'The bitch,' said Sarah.

'She was,' said Charles.

'But you liked it?'

'I suppose I must have, or I wouldn't have put up with it for so long.'

'Was she very good-looking?'

'Yes, in a cold kind of way, although she had a wonderful sense of humour, and she could be kind when she wanted. And she had that way of walking as if she couldn't be bothered putting one foot in front of the other.'

'I'm so bored we may as well fuck.'

'Exactly.'

'I bet she smoked.'

'She did, like a chimney.'

'Gauloises?'

'How did you know?'

'Intuition,' said Sarah. 'She sounds like quite a handful.'

'You've no idea,' said Charles. 'It would usually be very late when she got back, three or four o'clock in the morning, often the birds would be singing, I remember, but I was always overjoyed to see her. She'd keep her dress on in bed. I loved that, and she did too, God knows why, and in the morning she'd lie in bed smoking, and reading the essay I'd written for her. If she didn't think it was good enough, she'd tell me off, and make me do it again.'

'Is that all?'

'Mostly, yes.'

'Mostly?'

'I can't tell you any more, Sarah, really I can't.'

'You can't stop now.'

'I'm too embarrassed.'

'Now I have to know.'

'A couple of times she tied me to the bed and beat me,' he said quickly, blushing with shame.

'She beat you?' Sarah said, astonished but also aroused to think of her manly husband surrendering in such a way. 'What with, a whip?'

'No, thank God,' said Charles. 'Once with a belt, and the other time with one of her shoes. A sandal.'

'A sandal?'

'Yes,' he said. 'A yellow sandal with little gold buckles. I've never forgotten it.'

'Was it sore?'

'Sorer than you'd imagine.'

'Where did she beat you?'

'Where do you think?'

'On your bottom?'

'Yes.'

'Your bare bottom?' she asked, laughter in her voice.

'If you must know, yes.'

'What did she tie you with?'

'The sash from her dressing-gown. She'd wind it round and round my wrists, then tie it to the bed.'

'Did she tie you tight?'

'Tight enough.'

'You couldn't escape?'

'I couldn't.'

'Even if you tried?'

'Even if I tried.'

'Did you beg her to untie you?' Sarah asked, excited by the thought.

'No.'

'Why not?'

'I couldn't.'

'Why couldn't you?'

'She gagged me.'

'She did not!'

'She did.'

'What with?'

'I can't believe I'm telling you this,' he said, hiding his head in his hands.

'But you are, and I want to know.'

'Her knickers,' he confessed, his blush spreading to his neck.

'You're joking.'

'I'm not,' he said, avoiding her gaze. 'She'd just take them off and push them into my mouth. Then she'd tie one of her stockings around my head to keep them in place.'

'She used her dirty knickers?'

'Yes.'

'The ones she'd just worn?'

'Yes.'

'And you just let her?'

'I loved her,' he said. 'I wasn't in my right mind.'

'Did she fuck you when you were like that?'

'Not straight away. She'd leave me for ages while she made calls or smoked and drank wine. Sometimes she'd put music on and dance by herself. She liked to look at me though, walk round the bed while she talked and laughed on her phone. Once she sat astride me and fucked me while she was talking, I think it was to another man. She came while she was talking, but I didn't, and she just got up and kept talking on her phone.'

'My God,' said Sarah. 'What else did she do?'

'That was about it,' said Charles. 'It was more about attitude than anything else. It's hard to explain, but she had this air about her that expected to be obeyed, and she had a thing about me being naked while she was dressed. She liked to undress me as soon as we were alone – if we were at her place she'd hide my clothes so I couldn't find them – and she'd keep her clothes on while we kissed and made love. I think it made her feel powerful. It certainly made her seem very powerful to me.'

'A Mistress with her slave?'

'We never used those words,' he said, 'but I suppose so, yes.'

'Did you really love her?'

'I believe I did. Either that or I was besotted, if there's a difference. She was in my mind every minute of the day, I couldn't eat or sleep for thinking about her. She even made me clean her flat and do her laundry, often with no clothes on. When we went out she didn't introduce me to her friends as her boyfriend, she introduced me as her "helper," or "my assistant." It was a kind of madness.'

'Love is truly a madness,' said Sarah, quoting Rosalind from As You Like it, 'and, I tell you, deserves as well a dark house and a whip as madmen do.'

'Never a truer word,' said Charles.

'Why haven't you told me about her before?'

'Why do you think?'

'I don't suppose it was your proudest moment.'

'Hardly,' he said.

'All the same, I'd liked to have known,' said Sarah, wondering how different her marriage might have been had she known about her husband's time with Caroline Webster.

'Sometimes I think I dreamed it,' Charles said.

'So what happened? How did it end?'

'She'd come back from her parties drunk and high, and we'd make love, but then she started not coming back, and I discovered she had other lovers, both men and women. I was terribly hurt, but she expected me to put up with it. "If you want to fuck me," she said, "you'll just have to join the queue."'

'Nothing if not honest.'

'I stopped seeing her,' said Charles. 'I had to. She was too much for me in every sense of the word, but I was heartbroken. I had to re-sit my exams that year, and I only just scraped through. She came to see me a few months after we'd split up. She was strangely kind. "I'm just checking you're okay," she said. "I could take you back if I wanted. I could snap my fingers, and you'd come running, but I'm fond of you, and I don't think I'm good for you, so I'm setting you free. Goodbye, Charles, and good luck." And that was that. It took me a long time to get over her, and I vowed never to risk myself like that again.'

'Never to be a woman's slave?'

'Yes.'

'Have you seen her since?'

'No, but sometimes I read about her in the newspapers. She's become a famous lawyer. A very good one, I believe. Human Rights, of all things.'

'If she had snapped her fingers, would you have come running?'

'I'm not sure I could have stopped myself.'

'Poor Charles,' said Sarah, stroking his hair. 'I must seem very tame in comparison.'

'Not in the slightest,' Charles said, leaping to her defence. 'You're kind and lovely, a better person in every way, believe me.'

'A good wife,' said Sarah, 'but dull.'

'You know that's not true.'

'And poor.'

'I've never cared about money, you know that too.'

'Only because you've always had it.'

'Isn't that the best thing about having money, never having to care about it?'

'I'll give you that one,' said Sarah, an expert in the matter. Growing up with a hard-working but low-earning single mother, she'd never been free of worries about money. 'So where does that leave us?'

'Don't ask me,' said Charles, defensive again. 'It was you who wanted to talk.'

'Yes, and I still do.'

'We've had out talk.'

'About the past, yes, but not the future.'

'The future?'

'I think we should make some changes, Charles.'

'Give it a break,' he said warily.

'I think we can move on from here, truly I do.

'Please, Sarah, I've had enough.'

'I'm not sure that's the right way to speak to your Mistress.'

'What do you mean?' he said, but she'd seen his quick glance, the flash of hunger in his eyes.

'You know perfectly well what I mean,' Sarah said, trusting her instincts. 'A slave should speak respectfully to his Mistress. He should be on his best behaviour, and show his best manners at all times. Anything less should be viewed as unsatisfactory. It should be deemed substandard, and open to correction.'

'Correction?' he said with a snort of laughter as if she was joking, but she wasn't joking, at least, not really.

'I'm serious, Charles.'

'You can't be.'

'Oh, but I am,' she said, folding her arms, and keeping her manner clipped and stern. 'And just to prove it, I have a request to make of you, a request I expect you to carry out without the slightest complaint.'

'Do you indeed?' said Charles, trying to laugh away her nonsense, but his laughter had a false ring to it.

'I do,' said Sarah, holding to her course. 'I want you to kneel.'

'Kneel?' he said, unable to hide the panic in his voice.

'Yes, at my feet,' she said, oddly calm. 'I think I'd like it if you did that, and I have a feeling you'd like it too.'

'I can't do that,' he protested.

'Of course you can,' she said. 'Just get down on your knees, it's not difficult. Anyone could do it.'

'It's ridiculous,' he said, wondering why he was even discussing it with her.

'Of course it is,' she said. 'That's what makes it fun. The great Charles Hunter on his knees before his wife. Who could imagine such a thing?'

'Stop it, Sarah,' he said, fighting his arousal, trying to sound forbidding and manly.

'Why?'

'Because I won't do it.'

'Actually, you will, Charles, or you'll be in trouble.'

'Trouble?' he said as if she'd gone mad.

'Yes,' said Sarah, holding to her course. 'Very serious trouble.'

'This isn't happening,' he said, feeling dizzy. 'It can't be.'

'I'm afraid it is, Charles,' she said sternly. 'Get on your knees.'

'I've told you, no.'

'Don't keep me waiting,' she said, strangely sure of getting her way. 'You'll only make me angry.'

Charles shook his head in an attempt to clear his brain. Of course he wouldn't kneel. Sarah truly was being ridiculous. He'd never do such a thing, it was out of the question, but there was something about her manner, the matter-of-fact certainty in her voice, that made his brain swim. And the third button on her blouse had come undone, and he glimpsed the pretty lace of her bra. And somehow her perfume smelled stronger, and the curve of her smile seemed both mocking and infinitely sweet. He told himself to get up from the couch and leave the room before this foolishness got the better of him, and he went to do exactly that, but then, with a roaring in his ears, he found himself sliding to his knees until his eyes were level with the glass of wine she was holding in her lap. When Sarah spoke he heard her voice as if in a dream.

'That's the way,' she said, her voice warmly encouraging. 'You'll feel better now. You're where you belong, Charles – at your Mistress' feet.'

Now that he'd obeyed, Sarah felt a sense of vertigo that verged on panic. She hadn't really expected him to obey and, now that he had, she felt the burden of having to decide what comes next. Taking a deep breath, she told herself to stay calm, and speak honestly. If she was going to take charge of her husband, she needed to talk openly and with assurance, live up to her daring and make him accept her authority as his Mistress.

'You can put your head on my lap if you want,' she told him, buying some time. 'I won't mind.'

Grateful for a place to hide, he laid his head on her lap so meekly she found it both touching and comical. Could it really be this easy, she wondered, to put a man on his knees? Could a wife become her husband's Mistress just by adopting a stern manner and issuing a few instructions? And was she playing a role, or was she expressing her true nature? Was this the true Sarah Hunter or just a piece of foolish play-acting? It was too soon to tell, but she was looking forward to finding out.

'There,' she said, stroking his hair tenderly. 'Things seem much clearer this way, don't you think, with you down there and me up here? Now we can have a proper talk. And do you know what I mean by that?' she added with a nervous laugh. 'It's the kind where I speak, and you listen. A proper Mistress-slave talk.'

He made a strange sound as if her attempt at humour had angered him, but he kept his eyes down, pressing his head harder into her fragrant lap, and Sarah, a little dizzy with power, began to speak.

'There's really nothing to worry about,' she told him, taking a drink of wine. 'Everyone knows strong and powerful men like to surrender from time to time, that judges and generals want women to whip and scold them. It's perfectly understandable, logical almost. They need to take a holiday from themselves, find out what it's like not to be in control. It's the oldest cliché in the book, but that doesn't mean it's not true.'

In fact Sarah wasn't sure she believed any of this, suspecting that men put out this myth in order to validate their submissive desires. If only strong and powerful men liked to submit then they must be strong and powerful too. But, if it helped Charles to accept his sexuality, and her authority over him, then she was willing to use the myth to re-assure him of his deep-rooted manliness.

'I'm sure there are tens of millions of men in the world who dream of surrendering to their wives and girlfriends,' Sarah continued. 'And why shouldn't they? The world might be a better place if they did, don't you think?'

He remained silent, but she hadn't expected him to answer.

'But what I really want to talk about is how this works from a woman's point-of-view,' she said, warming to her subject. 'While I tell you about that, why don't you make yourself useful and give my feet a rub? I've had a busy day, and my shoes are killing me.'

He lifted his head, a startled expression on his face, but he took one of her feet, shucked off her neat little shoe, and began kneading her nylon-clad sole.

'That's lovely, Charles,' Sarah said, thrilled by his obedience. 'Don't you dare stop. I'm sure they're smelly, but you'll just have to put up with it. Now, where was I?'

'The woman's point-of-view,' he said, a man in a dream.

'Yes, that was it,' she said, surprised he'd been so attentive. 'Think how it's been for me, particularly when the children were young. The sleepless nights, the school-runs, dance-classes, swimming-club, homework, and then there was having to get on with your parents and your snooty sister. Your family never took to me. Thank God your sister lives in Italy now, and your parents hated me.'

'They didn't hate you.'

'Well, if they didn't, they certainly never believed I was good enough for their son. How could I be, a working-class girl brought up by a single mother who worked in shops and bars and liked a good time? I had to work extra hard to prove how kind and good I was, how grateful I was for my good fortune, how thankful to be your wife. The house had to be immaculate, the girls had to be perfect, I had to be so happy and grateful every minute of the day. And even now, back at work, I'm nice to everyone, always smiling, never late or angry. I meet every deadline, so much so that I'm given the donkey-work the senior accountants can't be bothered doing.'

'You should stand up to them.'

'You try it,' she said, 'when you're the only female accountant in the company.'

'I never knew it was so bad.'

'It's just how it is for every woman,' she said, 'but you don't listen. Either that or you think I'm exaggerating. And don't forget my feet,' she said. 'I was enjoying that.'

He'd stopped massaging her foot to listen, and he went back to his work, spreading her toes gently apart one by one, and rubbing his thumbs over the warm silky nylon sheathing her foot.

'That's wonderful,' she sighed, closing her eyes in pleasure. 'You have a talent for this, Charles. I think it must feel natural for you to be on your knees at my feet. Oh yes, if I have any say in matters, you'll be doing much more of this.'

She enjoyed his massage for long moments, letting her power over him sink in, before resuming her talk.

'What I'm really saying, Charles, is that I might want to be your Mistress and, when you hide the way you do, you're not just denying yourself, you're denying me the right to have what I want, and that's really not fair, is it? It may not be what a woman's supposed to want, but it's really rather nice to be the one in charge. If it's fun for you to surrender power because you've always had it, think how much fun it is for me to take power when I've never had it, at least not in the way a man has power in the world. Do you understand what I'm saying?'

'Yes,' he said, still rubbing her pretty foot, 'I think I do.'

'The joy of transgression,' she murmured, luxuriating in his ministrations. 'Is that what it is, do you think?'

'Possibly,' he said, struggling to stop from looking up her skirt.

'Then don't be so ashamed of what you want.'

'Easy to say.'

'That's just pride talking.'

'Pride doesn't just go away,' he said. 'It's on the hard-drive.'

'Surely it makes it easier if you know I want it too.'

'It might, I suppose,' he said, still very uncomfortable talking about his long-hidden desires.

'Then here's what I propose,' she said, shucking off her shoe and giving him her other foot. 'Let's bring it all out into the open. I'll be your Mistress and you'll be my slave. I'll be the lady of the house, and you'll be my house-servant. You've nothing better to do just now, and we need a cleaner, so it makes sense all round, don't you think?'

'A cleaner?'

'Yes,' she said. 'Is that a problem?'

'No,' he lied, shaken by the thought of occupying such a lowly position.

'I'm glad to hear it,' said Sarah. 'It's an honourable enough profession. My mother cleaned for people when she wasn't working in bars or waiting tables. It's how she fed me, and put clothes on my back, and helped me through university.'

'If it's what you want,' he said, submissive arousal spreading through his senses. He could do an hour of housework every day, of course he could. Where was the harm in that?

'I think it is what I want, Charles. It was lovely to come home this evening to a clean house and well-behaved husband, and so, yes, I'd like you to be my cleaner and housekeeper from now on.'

'Not all the time, surely?'

'I hadn't really thought, but why not?' she said, pleased that he seemed to be agreeing to her proposal. 'At least until you get another job.'

'That might take a while.'

'Then so much the better,' she said, smiling and pressing her nylon-clad foot against his face in a way that delighted his trembling heart. 'Congratulations, Charles, you've found a new job. Just think of the fun we'll have. I'll be your bossy, stuck-up Mistress, and you can be my manservant, my down-trodden slave, but I'm warning you – if you're going to be my housekeeper, you'd better be a good one. I won't tolerate laziness, or put up with shoddy work. And I'll wear my sexiest skirts and dresses, slips and heels too, I imagine. That'll keep you in your place, I'm sure. And maybe I'll make you take your clothes off while I stay dressed, just like Caroline Webster. I'll strut about the house telling you what to do, and you'll have no choice but to obey. Do this, do that, I'll say, and hurry up about it. If I've read this right, it's what you've always wanted, so don't be a coward, Charles. Let's give it a try at least, break the rules for once in our lives. Why shouldn't we? Life's too short apart from anything else. It can be our gift to each other, a reward for long-service. Say yes, Charles, go on.'

Sarah was surprised by how much she wanted him to agree. In a few short minutes she'd talked more openly and truthfully about sex than she had in the whole of their marriage, and she longed for something different, for some fun and mischief to come into their lives.

'Do we have to decide now?' Charles said, experiencing an alarming yet deliciously pleasurable drowning feeling.

'Now's as good a time as any, don't you think?' Sarah said, tapping her foot against his chin, her painted toe-nails gleaming beneath the nylon of her hose. 'While the mood's upon us.'

'C-can't we think about it?'

'If I know you, that could take years,' said Sarah, determined to have her way. 'No, Charles, I think we should strike while the iron's hot, and if you can't decide, then I'll decide for you. That might be best anyway, don't you think? I'm your Mistress, after all, and I shouldn't need your agreement.'

He tried to summon a response, but she didn't wait for him to answer.

'Now that I think of it,' she said, racing on, 'it's only right that I decide. So this is what's going to happen, are you ready to listen?'

He stared up at her, a wonder in his eyes, but she just laughed and said, 'You look very at home down there, I must say. It suits you, kneeling at my feet. I think you may have found your true place in life. Isn't life funny? After all these years of competing and winning and being the top-man it turns out you're happiest on your knees.'

He tried to speak but once more he couldn't make a sound. Sensing his helplessness, Sarah laughed, and said, 'Kiss my foot, Charles, I know you want to.'

Astonished, he made a sound like a cough. Her laughter infuriated him, and he'd never kissed her foot – and he was damned if he'd start now.

'Honestly, Charles,' she said, 'you're such a coward.'

He gave a shiver, fearing suddenly that he was in great danger, that if he gave in to her now there would be no going back.

'And what's this I see?' Sarah said, pushing her foot against the outline of his erection beneath his trousers. 'If you're not careful you'll burst out of your trousers. So, come on, Charles,' she said, lifting her foot to his mouth, and wiggling her toes insolently. 'Just one kiss to show you love me, and agree to be my slave. You can do it, I know you can. Just one teeny-tiny little kiss, that's not too much to ask, is it?'

He tried not to, he strove with every ounce of his strength, but he was in the grip of a force far greater than his volition and, before he could stop himself, he was lavishing adoring kisses on her nylon-sheathed foot, loving its silky warmth as well as its faint smell of sweat and shoe leather.

'That's what I like to see,' she said, hugely aroused by her victory, and surprised by the depth of his passion. 'Now we've had our little talk, I'm going to have all the fun of being the Mistress of the house, and you'll have the pleasure of being my obedient slave. I'm sure you're looking forward to it already, I know I am, and I don't see why it should be difficult. I mean, what could be simpler? I'll give you your instructions, and you'll do what I tell you, or else.'

Or else. My God, thought Sarah, where had that come from? Was she dreaming? Had she lost her mind?

'Not that I know what "or else" means,' she said, earthing her excitement by talking honestly. 'At least not yet, but I'm sure we'll find out as we go along. I might not be much good at this to start with, so you'll have to be patient with me, but I'm a quick learner, and I'm certain before too long I'll be the haughty, stuck-up Mistress you've always dreamed of, and you have dreamed of it, haven't you, Charles?'

Pressing his cheek against her ankle, he gave a heavy sigh.

'Tell the truth, Charles,' she said sternly. 'This won't work if you don't, and I won't permit any more hiding – that's all over and done with – and so I'll ask again. You've always dreamed of being my slave, haven't you?'

'Yes,' he confessed from the depths of his being.

'Then I'll do everything I can to make your dream come true,' Sarah told him, strangely moved by their exchange which seemed to carry the weight of a vow. 'So, then, what do you say?'

'Th-thank-you, Mistress.'

'You're very welcome,' she said, glorying in her ascendancy. 'You never know your luck, I may even give Caroline Webster a run for her money. You'd like it if I did, wouldn't you?'

'Yes,' he said, deeper under her spell.

'I thought you might,' she said. 'Now, Charles, you've kissed my foot very nicely,' she added, her senses on fire as she slid her tight suit skirt further up her thighs, parting her legs in a way that felt delightfully unladylike. 'And as a reward, there's somewhere else I'd like you to kiss, I'm sure you know where I mean.'

His heart pounding, Charles placed his head beneath the scented canopy of her skirt, and worshipped his lovely Mistress for all he was worth.

OVER THE next few weeks the transition from wife and husband to Mistress and slave happened very quickly and proved remarkably easy and enjoyable, particularly for Sarah who took an almost child-like delight in her new role as the lady of the house. The play-acting required amused her greatly – she often wondered if she was acting at all as she'd taken so naturally to her role – and the house resounded to the sound of her happy laughter. It was harder to tell if Charles was happy as he went about his work with a gravity that amused Sarah, and made her think of him as her stern and somewhat gloomy butler. Ordinarily, Charles had a lively sense of humour but, now a slave, he'd become too pre-occupied with sex and submission to find anything funny. His role as Sarah's slave seemed to possess him entirely, and he soon developed an almost monkish air of duty and devotion.

On the face of it, it was a simple enough arrangement. Sarah told Charles what to do, and he carried out her instructions in a state of shamed and helpless arousal, but their new arrangement wasn't entirely without its problems, particularly in the hour or so after Sarah got back from work.

They were both quite reserved by nature, and each time Sarah arrived home they went through a dance of stilted chat and awkward glances that prevented them from easily taking up their roles, but Sarah was an intelligent, resourceful woman, and she tackled the problem with her usual clear-headedness. Instead of entering the house with her key, she took to ringing the doorbell instead, and waiting for Charles to let her in as if he really was her butler, and woe betide him if he took too long to answer the door. She was very specific about the words he must use each evening to greet her. 'Welcome home, Mistress,' he'd have to say, his cheeks red with embarrassment, and his soul ascending to heaven. Their roles thus clearly and instantly defined, he would then follow his Mistress into the small cloakroom off the hall, which Sarah now referred to as the 'decompression chamber,' where he would take her coat and hang it up before kneeling at Sarah's feet with his head bowed. Sarah would stand above him for long moments, letting the strains of her day at work slowly fade as her power over him sank into their hearts and minds, before finally speaking.

'Well, now, Charles, your Mistress is home at last and ready to take charge of you. Are you happy to see her?'

'Yes, Mistress,' he'd say, a tremble in his voice. After waiting for her all day, dreaming of her, he'd be beside himself with excitement.

'Very good,' she'd say. 'It's lovely to be home and have you kneel in welcome. Are you truly my slave, Charles?'

'Yes, Mistress.'

'Then I accept your service.'

At this point a tremor would usually pass through him. On the rare occasions when this didn't happen, Sarah felt a sense of loss as if he wasn't sufficiently excited by her presence, and she would determine to be unusually strict with him for the rest of the evening.

'Is my meal ready?' she'd often say.

'Yes, Mistress?'

'Is my house clean and tidy?'

'Yes, Mistress.'

'In that case,' she might say, putting one foot elegantly in front of the other, 'you may kiss my shoe.'

In a fever of arousal, Charles would immediately bow his head and lavish adoring kisses on her elegant court shoe.

'Enough,' she'd say, raising the hem of her smart suit skirt, and speaking in her haughtiest manner. 'Now you may kiss my knee.'

She'd look down with satisfaction as he pressed his mouth to her nylon-clad knees, a lost look in his eyes. If she was in a generous mood, she'd raise her skirt a little higher so he could kiss the pretty lace hem of her underskirt. She knew the effect this had on him, and she'd laugh to hear him groan in arousal. Usually she'd stop him after a few kisses, content to have put him under her spell, and established their roles for the rest of the evening, but sometimes her own arousal got the better of her, and she'd take down her panties and hose and let him push her up against the hanging jackets and raincoats to worship between her legs, a man possessed by a never-ending hunger.

And it didn't take long for her to insist on Charles dressing smartly as her manservant. He'd ceased to shave since leaving work, and liked to slouch around the house in old jeans and flannel shirts, happy to take a break from the corporate uniform of suit and tie. After a few days of this, Sarah took him aside and informed him very firmly that she expected her slave to be smartly dressed and clean-shaven at all times, and she told him exactly what she wanted him to wear – black trousers with black shoes and a white shirt. She didn't insist on a tie, and she didn't want him in a jacket as that made him look too important, too much like his previous self, but she did insist on his shirt being neatly pressed and his shoes polished to a shine. As uniforms go, it was fairly casual, but Sarah thought he looked good in it, and she was convinced his smart appearance sparked a greater attentiveness in his attitude, and helped him embrace his position as her domestic slave. 'I much prefer you dressed like this,' she told him. 'It's a matter of respect. No matter what, a slave should always look his best for his Mistress.'

It was silly, she knew, and it was an act, but it worked and that was good enough for her.

But if Sarah had found a simple and effective routine to overcome shyness, and quickly establish her authority, she then encountered a much trickier problem – Charles' over-eagerness to please.

Charles had taken to his new life as her slave with a hunger that bordered on obsession. After hiding his desires for so many years, living as Sarah's servant woke in him not only an endless need to please his Mistress in whatever ways he could, but also a renewed sexual vigour more in keeping with a man twenty years his junior. Sarah felt it too, tuning in to Charles' submissive arousal, and feeding on the charged eroticism of sadomasochism. Just as Charles took endless delight in submission, Sarah found a rich and playful joy in wielding power. It was as if a miracle had taken place, and their middle-aged selves had been replaced by eager, young lovers.

Charles bought Sarah gifts nearly every day – flowers, chocolates, perfume and expensive wines as well as elegant clothes and underwear he found for her online. Already a good cook, he bought cookery books to extend his repertoire, and provide him with ever more delicious recipes to cook for Sarah. And then he'd ask her what shows she'd like to see, what concerts or films. And then it would be holidays, and he'd show her brochures, and quiz her about where she'd most like to go. On top of all that, he'd want to talk to her about this, that and everything. She had a certain sympathy with this, understanding that, like countless millions of housekeepers before him, he'd been on his own all day with no-one to talk to, and so, to begin with at least, Sarah put up with his chatter, but it soon became tiresome, and she found herself wondering how she could curb his eagerness without lessening his devotion.

And the same was true with sex. Every night, almost delirious with desire, Charles made love to her. His passion was infectious and Sarah returned it but, much as she enjoyed sex with him, she didn't want it every night, and she knew it should be on her terms, not his, and yet it was no easy matter to inform him of this without diminishing his ardour which would, in turn, weaken her control over him. He may have become her slave, but his feelings were still raw and fragile, and she knew she had to be careful with his training. She was greatly taken with her new life as his Mistress, and she didn't want to risk losing it.

And so Sarah took her time, working through a number of different strategies in her head before gradually introducing them into their relationship. Day by day, she took small steps that pushed Charles further and deeper under her control. If there was the slightest crease in a blouse or skirt, she'd hand it back to him and make him iron it again, warning him that she wouldn't tolerate such poor service, and in the evenings she took to using him as her footstool while watching television or working on her lap-top, and she'd often have him massage her feet while she lazed on the couch drinking wine and talking to friends and colleagues on her phone, something that gave her particular pleasure, and inflamed Charles' submissive arousal.

And then Sarah came up with the idea of a weekly ritual she hoped might take her control over Charles to an even higher level. She called this ritual 'Mistress-Time.' Every Sunday evening at exactly eight o'clock, she'd take Charles into her study where she instructed him to take off all his clothes, and kneel at her feet while she sat fully clothed in her armchair, a queen on her throne. In a daze, Charles would obey at once, his hands trembling with excitement as he undressed in front of his Mistress' sternly mocking gaze. And for Sarah, remaining dressed while Charles was naked aroused her deeply, and greatly increased her sense of power and authority as she reviewed his past week's performance, and told him what she expected from him in the week ahead.

These sessions gave her the opportunity to modify Charles' behaviour, and mould his service more closely to her tastes, but she was always careful to praise him before pointing out any improvements he could make.

On their third Mistress-Time she felt confident enough to address the problem of his over-eagerness to please, and his excessive talkativeness.

'I want you to know I'm very pleased with you, Charles,' she began. 'You've had another excellent week, I'm happy to say. You've been polite and attentive at all times, the meals you've prepared have been delicious, the house is spotless, and my clothes and underwear are laid out neatly on the bed for me every morning. In many ways, I couldn't be happier, and I'm delighted with the new course our marriage has taken. I never dreamed we'd live like this – it really does feel like a reward for long-service – and I very much want it to continue.'

'Thank-you, Mistress,' he said, as lifted by her praise as he was beguiled by her haughty manner.

'And I take it you also want to keep on living like this?'

'Yes, Mistress,' he said, his voice catching with emotion. He was astonished by the pleasure he felt serving Sarah – a pleasure so pure and intense he often felt he was dreaming – and he didn't want it to stop.

'Very good, Charles, but I have a few suggestions as to how you may improve your service,' Sarah said, pleased to see him come fully erect. 'It's important you don't view my suggestions as criticism, but merely as pointers towards becoming an even better slave. Can you do that?'

'Yes, Mistress.'

'And are you ready to pay attention?'

'Yes, Mistress,' he said, hugely aroused by her business-like manner.

'Very good, then I shall begin. It's very kind of you to buy me gifts. I appreciate the time and thought you put into choosing them, but I can't help feeling it's presumptuous of a slave to buy presents for his Mistress, particularly intimate items such as underwear and clothes, pretty and elegant as they invariably are. And so, from now on, I will tell you what gifts you may buy for me, and I will buy my own clothes and underwear. I may from time to time allow you to buy me new panties or nylons, or a new dress or shoes, but it will only be as a reward for your good behaviour. For example, if I am particularly pleased with you, or perhaps if it is your birthday, I may allow you to buy me a gift as a token of your love and respect. And another thing – I will also decide on the menu for the week, although you will be permitted to make suggestions. From this moment on, these will be my choices, Charles, not yours. Am I understood?'

'Yes, Mistress,' he said, but she'd seen the hurt look in his eyes.

'Now, you mustn't be upset, Charles. We can't have a slave deciding what his Mistress wears, can we? Of course not, that would be entirely the wrong way round. I may be free to decide what you wear as my slave, but on no account may you have any say over what I wear as your Mistress.'

'I'm sorry,' he said, so sweetly crushed he feared he might faint.

'That's quite alright,' she said, greatly enjoying her absurd performance, and the power it gave her to order their lives as she saw fit. 'You were merely trying to please me, a fault entirely in the right direction. And, really you know, your service and submission as my slave are by far the best gifts you can give me. All I'm asking is that you take a few steps back, and wait until I tell you before buying me anything. I'm sure you can do that.'

'Yes, Mistress,' he said uncertainly. He loved buying gifts for her, looking for clothes and underwear he thought she might like, and he was going to miss serving her in that way.

'I'm sure it will give you even more pleasure knowing anything you do buy for me will be my choice, not yours.'

'Yes, Mistress,' he said, already infected by a new strain of submissive arousal.

'That way your gifts will be what I want to receive, not what you want to give and, mark my words, there is a world of difference between the two.'

'Yes, Mistress.'

She smiled to see his erection leap, and touch against his flat stomach. She'd insisted he keep up his visits to the gym, and he swam fifty lengths in the nearby public swimming-baths three times a week. She wanted a fit and healthy as well as an attractively slim slave, and she was pleased by his athletic appearance. 'God, it's fun to have a naked man at my feet,' she thought, her lazy arousal sweetened by the thrill of power.

'And the same goes for theatre tickets and holidays,' she told him, hitting her stride. 'I'll inform you what shows I want to see, or what holiday destinations I prefer. And not only that, I'll decide if you will accompany me or not.'

This one took her by surprise. An entirely new thought, it had dropped into her head from out of the blue, but it made her heart leap with excitement – a sure sign she was going to enjoy this new freedom.

'A Mistress shouldn't go out with her slave. It's hardly appropriate. She will have others to accompany her to parties and shows, people she considers to be her equals. I think it's important you come to terms with that. It's an important stepping-stone towards a stronger and more truthful bond between us as Mistress and slave. You have to understand that I truly am your superior, Charles. I know that's entirely wrong by any reasonable way of thinking, but all the same that's how things are. Whatever this thing is we've found, it goes beyond reason and sets its own rules. What must be must be. Certainly, I'm finding it easier with every passing day to view you as my inferior and my subordinate, and no longer as my husband and equal.'

She saw him wince in pain. It had been a harsh thing to say, but it gave her pleasure to say it, and a shockingly profane image suddenly invaded her mind, bringing with it a jolt of dark arousal. She saw herself dressed in a lovely dress opening the front-door to a handsome man – her date for the night while Charles stayed at home as her slave and housekeeper. Charles was present in the image but not visible, a figure hiding in the shadows of the hallway as she welcomed her lover with an embrace, whispering in his ear, 'I've been waiting for you, darling, waiting and waiting.'

'Of course I'll take you with me from time to time,' Sarah said, 'particularly when we visit friends or family who know us as a couple – I don't suppose we can frighten all the horses – but I want you to get used to spending evenings alone. You may wait up for me, of course, and attend me when I return.'

Attend me?

'I don't mean to be cruel,' she continued, suspecting that was exactly what she intended, and noting with interest that he was still fully erect. 'I'm only trying to be a proper Mistress to you, I hope you understand that.'

'Yes, Mistress,' he said, jealousy and alarm feeding his twisted arousal.

'So, then, to recap,' Sarah said, satisfied that real progress had been made. 'Just as you'll no longer presume to buy me gifts, neither will you presume to be my companion for the evening, or on holiday for that matter – although I may let you travel as my servant. Perhaps, if I hire a house or cottage, you can come as my housekeeper and chalet-maid – now, there's an idea, I could buy you a dress and make you into my lady's-maid – but that will be my decision, not yours. In these matters, as in all else, you will be instructed, not consulted, as befits a slave. Is that clear?'

'You should go on the stage,' Sarah told herself, struggling not to laugh out loud at her outrageous performance.

'Yes, Mistress,' said Charles, utterly enthralled.

'The more we live like this,' she said, a playful warmth in her eyes, 'the more I realise it's real and not a game. I expect you feel the same.'

'Yes, Mistress,' he said, barely able to breathe.

'It's like magic,' said Sarah, genuinely amazed at how quickly their lives had changed, and at how easy she found it to be his selfish and bossy Mistress. 'I had no idea it was even possible to take charge of a man, and I never dreamed it could be so much fun. I don't think I could stop now even if I wanted to. It's almost like the magic has a mind of its own. What do you say to that?'

Charles wanted to speak but he could think of nothing to say. Thrilled by her confident manner, and by the sight of her shapely nylon-clad knees just inches from his face, he experienced once more the lovely drowning feeling that always accompanied submission to Sarah. He felt frightened and exposed and very ashamed of himself, but he also felt a profound happiness that verged on spiritual joy.

'There's one more thing,' she informed him, aroused by his silence. 'I don't always feel like talking when I get home from work. I like to hear your news, of course I do, and tell you mine, but I'd prefer some quiet time on my own when I first get in. And so, once you've answered the door to me and hung up my coat, I don't want to hear another word until I tell you. A simple rule might be – don't speak unless spoken to, or, slaves should be seen and not heard. Do you agree to that?'

'Yes, Mistress,' he said, helpless against her.

'That's wonderful, Charles,' she told him with her creamiest smile, the same one she used to give his mother when she came to visit. 'This has been a splendid Mistress-Time. Keep this up, and I'll have no choice but to consider myself the luckiest woman in all the wide world.'

IN BED Sarah struggled to find an equally effective way to control his ardour, partly because she often shared it, and very much enjoyed sex with her enamoured slave. She may have been his Mistress, but it was lovely to be so passionately desired, and yet she wanted to take charge in bed as she had in all other aspects of their marriage. She wanted the power to deny him.

Finally, after many nights of being lovers, she pushed him away when he turned to her.

'No, Charles, not tonight,' she told him.

'I love you,' he told her, his eager cock pressing into her side.

'I know you do,' she said warmly. 'And I love the way you want me – I don't wish that ever to stop – but I'm not like you, I don't need sex every night. You're wearing me out, and apart from anything else, you've made me sore down here. It's a lovely kind of sore, but it's painful all the same.'

'I'm so sorry,' he said instantly contrite. 'I had no idea.'

'Don't be sorry,' she said. 'It's wonderful having this after being married for so long. Not many couples find it again, I'm sure, but I'm your Mistress and I should decide when we have sex, don't you think?'

'Yes, Mistress,' he said, even more aroused.

'And it's not as if you have to do without,' she said, a mischievous edge to her voice.

'What do you mean?' he said, feeling a new excitement.

'Get out of bed and you'll see.'

'Get out of bed?'

'Yes.'

'Why?' he said, confused.

'Just do as you're told.'

He got out of bed and stood naked, his erection pointing skywards with a hopeful vigour that made Sarah laugh.

'Look at you,' she said through laughter. 'Such a sweet and willing slave.'

'What now?' he said, feeling so foolish and exposed he covered up his arousal with his hands.

'Take your hands away,' she said. 'I like to see.'

He took his hands away, and stood helpless before her.

'Touch yourself,' she commanded. 'Make yourself harder.'

He took hold of his cock and stroked it lightly, finding such pleasure he gasped, and bent forward as if he might come there and then.

'You can stop now,' she said.

Obeying instantly, he let go of his cock which had grown painfully erect.

'Now go into the shower room,' she instructed him.

'The shower-room?' he said, his head spinning.

'Stop repeating everything I say,' she said, still laughing. 'On you go, or I'll change my mind, and then you'll be sorry.'

Sarah smiled to see him go into the shower-room. Was there nothing he wouldn't do for her?

'Go over to the laundry-basket,' she called to him.

In the shower-room, Charles approached the laundry-basket. 'If you look in the basket,' he heard her call, 'you'll find my knickers and tights.' He rummaged in the basket and there, beneath her slip and blouse, he found her panties balled up inside a pair of sheer, dark tights. His heart pounding, he took the delicate garments from the basket.

'Have you found them?' she called.

'I've found them,' he replied, a croak in his voice.

'Then bring them back to bed with you.'

He came into the bedroom holding her delicate underthings, a priest with his offering.

'Get in,' Sarah said, holding back the duvet.

He lay beside her, and went to take her in his arms.

'No, Charles, I've told you,' she said firmly. 'Lie on your back instead.'

When he obeyed, she lay against him, her head close to his on the pillow, her mouth by his ear.

'Let's see what we've got here,' she said, taking the panties and hose from him. Without looking she untangled her panties from her hose and held them to his face. He started in shock, but she'd expected that, and she pushed her knickers more firmly against his mouth and nose.

'There,' she said. 'That's what you need.'

'What are you doing?' he protested, his shocked and muffled voice making her want to laugh.

'Keep quiet,' she instructed him. 'And keep still.'

She held him like that for long moments, whispering soothingly in his ear, 'Deep breaths,' and 'that's a good boy,' until she felt him settle and lie still, sedated by her woman's scent.

'You can smell me, can't you, Charles?' she said, delighted by the success of her ruse. 'You can smell me on my panties … My soft, lacy knickers … What a lucky slave you are … Deep breaths now … That's it … That's the way … Nice and deep.'

Feeling as if he was falling, Charles breathed in her musky scent along with the faint tang of her pee, finding it not dirty but glorious, the scents binding him more closely to her, not just as his wife and Mistress, but also as his animal partner in life. Enraptured, he felt himself fall into a trance as if she was holding a wad of chloroform to his nose.

'This is for you,' she said, putting him under. 'For being such a good and obedient slave.' He gave a groan, and pushed his face deeper into her panties.

'You like that, don't you?' she taunted him. 'My pretty knickers so soft against your face … My smell on them … My most private smell.'

He made a guttural noise that she knew meant yes.

'I have another treat for you,' she whispered. 'Something else I'm sure you'll like. Are you ready?'

'Yes,' he gasped.

'I beg your pardon.'

'Yes, Mistress.'

'Then here you are,' she said, placing the silken bundle of her tights over his erection, and rubbing him slowly, maddeningly through the soft nylon. 'The tights I wore today … All day … Standing, sitting, walking … Crossing my legs, uncrossing them … Under my skirt … Against my legs, over my panties … Pulling them down in the bathroom, pulling them up again … They feel good, don't they, Charles, so soft and smooth?'

Hugely aroused by her sly whispers, he said nothing, just sighed in delight, and pushed his cock against her nylons.

'What more could a slave want?' she goaded him, 'but his Mistress' pretty underwear?'

She rubbed a little harder, and then took her hands away.

'You do it,' she instructed him. 'A Mistress shouldn't have to do all the work.'

Her puppet now, he held her panties against his nose and, with his other hand, pressed her silky hose around his erection.

'Oh, God,' he muttered, his eyes closing in delight. 'Oh, God.'

'That's good, Charles,' she praised him. 'That's what I want to see.'

'I love you,' he said helplessly.

'A slave can't help loving his Mistress,' she said, her voice softly hypnotic. 'That's it, Charles, deep breaths … That's the way … And another … Good boy … I've caught you in my silken trap and I'll never let you go … I'll keep you as my prisoner … You can try to escape if you want but you'll never be free … Never ever … Come for me now … Come in my stockings.'

He moaned as if he was in pain, but his hand began to move faster. Excited by his surrender, Sarah slid her hand between her legs, and began to finger herself, her cunt slick with arousal. It was lovely to take control of him like this, put him under in a way that felt both inevitable and final.

Charles had masturbated countless times in his life, particularly as a younger man when he couldn't get sex out of his head, and more recently during the day, looking to rid himself of the arousal he felt living as a slave, but he'd never done it in front of Sarah, or anyone else for that matter. He'd always considered it a private and slightly shameful act, and he felt very ashamed of himself now, but he could do nothing to stop himself. He was far too deep under her woman's spell, overwhelmed by her power and beauty.

'Faster, Charles,' Sarah said, sensing his orgasm was close. 'This is what we'll do when I can't be bothered having sex with you. I'll give you my undies instead, my worn tights and dirty panties. We'll call it 'panty-sex,' I think, as good a name as any, wouldn't you say? I'm sure you'll come to love it as much as real sex. Who knows, maybe the day will come when it's the only kind of sex I'll allow you? Poor Charles,' she taunted. 'No more sex for him. Only real men deserve real sex, not panty-lovers, not slaves … Slaves

have to make do with panty-sex ... That's all they deserve, all they can expect
...'

Wounded by her words, yet hugely aroused, Charles cried out in an ecstasy of joy and shame as he emptied himself into her silky nylons

His loud cries prevented him from hearing Sarah's secret little cry of joy, and he lay in a daze as she whispered in his ear, 'Go to sleep, now, Charles ... Sleep, and dream of all the things I can do with you ... All the cruel and lovely games we can play ... Just you wait, my love ... Just you wait ...'

IN THE days and weeks that followed Sarah still allowed Charles to make love to her, but not nearly so frequently for she found a special joy in limiting him to panty-sex, and she particularly enjoyed telling him fantasy stories to increase his arousal, and deepen his servitude. It became her way of trying out new ideas, and finding out what aroused him most powerfully. And she found out a great deal about herself too, for she uncovered some very dark and hidden alleyways in her own erotic imagination. Rather to her surprise, she found she had a dirty and inventive mind when it came to dreaming up scenarios of surrender and humiliation and, while tormenting Charles with tales of cruelty certainly deepened his submission, it also woke in her, not just a more dominant streak, but also a playfulness that made even the most degrading scenario seem almost innocent. More than anything, Sarah found her new relationship with Charles to be the greatest fun. She thought of it as an adult form of 'doctors and nurses' and other childish dressing-up games, and she gave thanks for it. By some miracle, she'd rediscovered the joy of 'play,' and she felt younger and stronger for having it in her life. Emboldened by fun and freedom, she ventured happily beyond the walls of convention. A whole new world was opening up before her, and she was going to explore every land, and sail every sea.

In bed at night, a filthy-minded Scheherazade, she whispered outlandish tales of power and punishment into Charles' ear. She most enjoyed describing the parties she'd hold where Charles served as butler to her elegant guests, telling him he'd have to take their coats and serve drinks from a tray while she danced and flirted with other men. The thought of going with other men thrilled her, and she couldn't help but notice how much it aroused Charles. 'Of course I'll dance with other men,' she'd taunt him. 'I'm your Mistress, I can do what I like.'

Other nights she'd whisper to him about the holidays she'd take with Charles travelling as her servant, frequently as a uniformed lady's-maid who'd have to curtsey to her Mistress before helping her to dress or undress, an embellishment that invariably aroused Charles to the point of no return. 'Oh, dear, Charles,' she'd say once he'd come in her nylons. 'How much you like being my lady's-maid. I'll have to make it happen soon, won't I? It would be unkind of me not to.'

And she'd often taunt him about making him sign over all his money to her, as well as his share of the house, so that she would have everything, and he'd have nothing. 'I'll divorce you then, Charles,' she'd say as he neared orgasm, 'but I'll keep you on as my slave, make you sleep in the little room at the back of the kitchen. You'll be my scullery-maid. Then it really won't be a game any more, will it? It'll be real and inescapable. You'd better mind how you go then,' she'd warn him, 'or I'll throw you out into the street, or find an even crueller woman and give you away to her. I'll find a real man, a better man, and forget all about you.'

As she told these stories she felt a wildness between her legs that possessed her, and drove her to even wilder flights of fancy. One night when Charles was more that usually aroused, she teased him about his liking for her underwear. 'I think you love my panties more than you love me,' she taunted him, 'but you can't help yourself, can you? You'd do anything for a pair of my knickers, give up everything to lie in bed with my undies and have me whisper dirty stories in your ear. Filthy, shameful stories that no self-respecting man would want to hear, but then you're not a man any more. You're a panty-slave now. Well, you are, aren't you?'

'Yes,' he gasped, her knickers tight against his nose.

'Then say it,' she said. 'Make your confession.'

'I'm your p-panty-slave,' he stammered, utterly lost.

'Now we know the truth,' she said, cupping his balls while he crushed her nylons around his erection. 'But what am I going to do with my panty-slave now it's all out in the open? What would he like me to do, I wonder?'

He made a choking sound, and she squeezed his balls to put him deeper under her sway.

'I think I know what you'd like, Charles,' she said, her voice warm and goading. 'Since you like my knickers so much, perhaps I'll let you wear them.' As soon as she'd said the words, he gave a loud groan, shaking his head from side to side but trembling as if an electrical current had passed through him. 'You can shake your head all you like,' she teased him, delighted to have stumbled on such a simple and amusing way to take advantage of him, 'but I know it's what you want. Oh, yes, Charles, I know you want to wear my panties. My lacy panties. My woman's panties. My dirty panties. In that case, I'll give you these knickers to wear in the morning. I'm going to, Charles, I promise, maybe every morning from now on, who knows? Just think, you'll soon be wearing my panties. How soft they'll feel against your skin, and how silly you'll look in them. It's going to happen, Charles, I give you my word. I'm going to make you into my panty-slave, not just for a night or a day, but for the rest of your life.'

AND SARAH was as good as her word. In the morning, when Charles rose first to prepare breakfast, she was quick to remind him of her promise.

'Aren't you forgetting something?' she said as he reached into the drawer that contained his boxer shorts.

'I don't … I'm not …' he blustered, fear in his eyes.

'Oh, stop it,' she said, amused by his attempt to escape his fate. 'You know perfectly well you'll do what you're told. And here they are,' she said, holding up her panties which she'd found in the bed beside her. They were full-cut, but very feminine in a dusty pink colour edged with lace. 'Put them on,' Sarah instructed him, the knickers dangling from the end of her finger, as mesmerising as a hypnotist's pocket-watch.

'I can't,' he protested.

'Oh, but you can,' she said, a hard look coming into her eyes. 'And you will.'

'They're too small,' he said, unable to take his eyes from the terrifying garment. 'They'll never fit.'

'I'll be the judge of that. Now put them on, Charles, before I get angry.'

Powerless against her, Charles went over to the bed and took the panties from her, their silken weightlessness thrilling his senses, and making him come partially erect.

'What do you say?' Sarah asked him.

'Th-thank-you,' he stuttered.

'Hurry up,' she said. 'You'll make me late.'

His hands trembling, and his cheeks burning with shame, Charles stepped into the panties, and pulled them up his legs.

'Actually, they fit you rather well,' said Sarah, pleased at how foolish and unmanly her husband looked in her knickers, and amused to see him hurry to put on his trousers to hide his shame. 'I like you like this,' she said as he buttoned up his smart white shirt. 'I don't know why, but it feels right to put you in panties. Maybe it's because you're not really a man any more, and don't deserve to dress like a man,' she added cruelly, her hand slipping between her legs. 'I've made up my mind,' she said as her pleasure mounted. 'You'll be wearing my knickers every day from now on. I'm going to insist on it. Aren't you a lucky slave? Well, aren't you?'

'Yes, Mistress,' he said, a tremble in his voice.

'Then go and make my breakfast. I'll be down in ten minutes.'

But Sarah stayed in bed much longer. Surprised by the absence of guilt or remorse, she lay back and recalled some of the cruel and mischievous games she played with her husband. Or were they games, she wondered? Perhaps her taunts had been true, and this was real now, and she truly had turned Charles into her slave. It was a preposterous thought but, as she showered and dressed and put on her make-up, she was possessed by a dreamy and pleasant arousal that stayed with her for the rest of the day.

And the same was true for Charles, although his arousal was much more troubled. He went about his day in a daze of shame and astonishment at his weakness, the woman's panties under his trousers an ever-present reminder of Sarah's power over him, yet he did not take off the knickers. He thought about it many times, and twice went upstairs to replace the panties with a pair of his boxer shorts, but he couldn't take them off. It thrilled him too much to be enslaved and imprisoned in such a way, and before long he began to look forward to Sarah giving him his panties for the day. It was such a silly thing, and yet it increased his submission tenfold, and opened the flood-gates to a new and much more extreme kind of play.

For, now that she'd put him in panties, Sarah began to experiment with other forms of dress-up. One night she put a little band with cat's ears over Charles' head, and made him keep it on all evening, telling him he was her pussycat. He felt angry and humiliated to be treated in such a way, but nonetheless he took it from her without complaint, secretly thrilled by the humiliation, particularly when she made him lie on the couch with his head in her lap while she stroked his hair, and called him 'puss' and 'kitten.'

A few nights later she looked out a little white apron from the back of a drawer in the kitchen, and tied it around his waist with a big bow at the back, and made him keep it on while he served her evening meal. It was a woman's apron, dainty and pretty with a delicate frill around its edge. She thought it looked pleasingly neat against his black trousers, and she made him wear it whenever she wanted to be particularly stern and dominant with him, something she wanted more and more as she grew into her role as his Mistress. Charles looked very unhappy when he wore it, cowed and ashamed, but she knew it aroused him deeply to wear such an effeminate and menial garment. 'It'll have to do for now,' she told him. 'Until I find you a proper maid's uniform.'

Sarah told herself it was only a little fun, yet the contempt she felt for Charles when he wore the apron was real and strong, and so arousing that, after her meal, she often made him stand facing the corner while she read her book or watched television. It was a punishment she remembered from her time in primary school and she knew Charles found it almost unbearably demeaning but, if he dared object, she'd simply tell him, 'It's your punishment for looking so silly in your apron, and for not being man enough to take it off.' She'd wait for long moments, giving him the chance to stand up to her, but he could never summon the strength, either that or her haughty manner aroused him too much for he'd always look away first before lowering his head in defeat. 'See what I mean,' she'd say. 'Now go to your corner, and stay there until I say otherwise.'

It gave her a dark joy to watch him go to his corner by the bookcase, and stand there with his hands clasped behind his back in the way she'd instructed him. Her gaze would often turn to her helpless slave with his red-cheeked face pressed to the wall, and the long, shaming bow of his apron hanging from his waist and, without him seeing, and very aroused by the sight of her enslaved husband, her hand would find its way beneath her skirt or dress.

And Sarah too began to dress more provocatively. She knew that the smart skirt suits and elegant blouses she usually wore to work played well to Charles' ideal of a dominant and successful woman, and she often didn't bother to change her clothes when she returned from work, but every now and then she took things further. Some evenings she'd take off her skirt and go about in just her tights and heels, amused by the nervous excitement this provoked in Charles. And she often took off her dress, or skirt and blouse, and went about in just her slip, knowing how much Charles loved her like that.

She also had a lovely white mini-slip that she wore from time to time. It barely reached past her bottom, and she always teamed it with her sheerest hose and matching white panties, making sure to allow Charles a glimpse of her panties whenever she sat down, or crossed her legs. His dazed expression brought her no end of amusement, and his lovestruck devotion invariably led to him falling to his knees, and begging to worship her. She usually let him, but not always. Sometimes it brought her a darker and deeper pleasure to deny him, and watch him suffer.

Some evenings she wore a black knee-length pleated skirt, liking the way it moved and swayed around her knees. She usually wore it with a pair of knee-high leather boots. To begin with she feared that wearing boots would make her into too much of a clichéd Mistress figure, but once she saw how much wearing boots increased her sexual power over Charles, she wore them more and more. Other nights she wore a full circle skirt fashioned in layers of tulle and net that made him mad for her, and once she dressed in a rock'n'roll skirt with a petticoat beneath, amused at the effect her full petticoat had on her husband. 'You can't wait, can you?' she teased her trembling slave. 'You can't wait to kneel at my feet and lose yourself under my petticoats. But take care, Charles. If you get too lost you may never find your way out of the woods, and you'll be my prisoner forever.'

One memorable evening she even put on the suspender belt and black seamed stockings he'd bought for her three Christmases ago, and which she'd never worn. She often wore stay-up stockings in summer, but she'd never liked wearing stockings with suspenders, disliking the bother of putting them on, and finding them uncomfortable when she did. But it was a different matter when she was doing it for her own pleasure. She paired the stockings with her highest heels and a black leather pencil skirt and a fitted black top. She put on long-sleeved black velvet evening gloves to add an extra touch of glamour, and her slave's reaction to her appearance didn't disappoint her. When she came into the kitchen and turned slowly to let him see the seams in her stockings, and how tightly the skirt fitted around her bottom, poor Charles could only stare like a fool.

'Can you guess what I'm wearing under my skirt?' she asked him, experiencing a delicious thrill of power.

'N-no,' he stammered.

'Oh, I think you can,' she said. 'I'm wearing the stockings and suspenders you bought for me. It's your reward for being a good and obedient slave, but you'd better make the most of it, Charles. I don't enjoy wearing suspenders, and it might be a very long time before I wear them again. So what do you say?'

'Thank-you, Mistress.'

'Would you like to see the tops of my stockings?'

'Y-yes.'

'I thought you might,' Sarah said, a mocking edge to her voice. 'Then, how about this – once you've served me my meal, and tidied the kitchen and finished the ironing, I'll let you see my stocking-tops, but only if your work's up to standard. Are we agreed?'

'Yes, Mistress.'

'Very good,' she said, sitting at table and tasting her wine which she found delicious. 'In that case you may serve my meal.'

Once she'd eaten, and Charles had finished his chores for the evening, he came into the living-room where Sarah was watching television, and stood anxiously, waiting for her to notice him.

'What is it now?' she said once her programme was over, sounding very bored with him.

'I've finished my work,' he said, a tremor in his voice.

'I'm pleased to hear it,' she said, getting to her feet. 'Then I suppose I'd better inspect your work.'

She took great pleasure in touring the house to inspect his housework, speaking always in a haughty, superior manner, and walking ahead of Charles as she led him from room to room so she could feel his eyes on her stocking-clad legs, and know he could hear the tormenting whisper of her skirt against her hose. The house was wonderfully clean and tidy, but she made sure to find fault here and there just for the fun of it, and to make him fear he may not receive his longed-for prize. By the time they returned to the living-room, Charles was shaking with arousal.

'The house is very tidy, but even so I don't think I can show you my stockings,' Sarah announced mischievously, refilling her wine glass and sitting in her armchair. 'Not because your work isn't good, but because I'm worried seeing my underwear might be too much for you.'

'Please,' he beseeched her, a dark hunger in his eyes.

'Are you begging me, Charles?'

'Yes.'

'Let me hear you, then.'

'I beg you, Mistress.'

'Very well,' she said, raising her skirt hem slowly. 'But just a very quick look. I don't want to give you a heart-attack.'

Sarah slid her skirt to the tops of her thighs, allowing him only the briefest glimpse of her stocking-tops and suspenders, before pulling down her skirt, and primly arranging its hem at her knees.

'There,' she said, amused by the pain such a brief glimpse of heaven had brought to his eyes. 'You've had your look. Do you feel better now?'

He made a sound like a cough, and the pain in his eyes seemed to deepen.

'Oh, dear,' she said in mock sympathy. 'I don't think you are better. In fact, I think showing you my stockings had only made you worse. Poor Charles, you look as if you need a drink.'

She saw a different hunger come into his eyes. Before she'd made him her slave, Charles had enjoyed a large whisky every night before bed, but it had been well over a month now since he'd enjoyed such a luxury.

'Would you, Charles?' she asked. 'Would you like a drink, perhaps a glass of your favourite Jameson's whisky?'

'Yes,' he said warily, suspecting a trap.

'I haven't allowed you a whisky or even a glass of wine for a very long time, have I?'

'No.'

'And all that time I've enjoyed wine with my meals, and often had another glass or two while I'm watching television or listening to music. I really am a cruel and heartless woman, you have to say.'

He nearly agreed with her, but thought better of it.

'I'm on the horns of a dilemma over this, Charles,' she said, a smile in her eyes as she drank her wine, relishing the freedom to enjoy what he could not have. 'Being a Mistress can create such quandaries, you've no idea. Let me explain,' she said, sitting back in her armchair and crossing her lovely legs. 'I know you'd love a whisky, and I'd like nothing more than to let you have one – goodness knows you've earned it – but then a Mistress really shouldn't drink with her slave. It sets the wrong example, and runs the risk of giving him ideas above his station, I'm sure you see my problem.'

Her lovely, full mouth curved in a smile, and Charles felt his temper rise. He knew she was playing with him, a cat with a bird, waking his hopes only to crush them again, but arousal overwhelmed his rage, and he stood silently before her, a helpless slave to her beauty. In the way he'd come to crave, he loved her for her cruelty, and longed for her to crush his pride beneath her absolute authority.

'I wonder,' she said, tapping a finger against her wine-glass as a new and thrillingly decadent idea took shape in her mind. 'There must be something I can do, don't you think? I'm an intelligent woman, I should be able to come up with a compromise. I know, let's try this,' she said with sudden energy. 'Go and get the bottle, and fetch a glass while you're at it. Hurry up,' she added impatiently, 'before I change my mind.'

When Charles returned with the whisky bottle, Sarah put down her wine-glass and took the heavy crystal glass from him, holding it in her elegantly gloved hand, and saying, 'You may do the honours. A good measure now.' Charles poured three fingers of whisky before replacing the top and putting the bottle down beside Sarah's wine-glass.

'I love the smell of whisky,' said Sarah, holding the glass to her nose, 'but I've never much liked the taste.' She took a sip and immediately made a face. 'And I still don't, but you love it, don't you?'

'I do,' he said, still suspecting a trap.

'I'm going to try something I've never done before,' she said, sliding her hips forward so that her leather skirt rode up her thighs allowing him to see the bands of darker nylon at the tops of her stockings. 'It might be a stupid idea, but I'm going to try it anyway. Kneel for me, Charles, kneel at my feet.'

His head spinning, Charles instantly obeyed, gazing in astonishment as Sarah tugged her skirt right to the tops of her thighs, and opened her legs, giving him an unobstructed view of her stocking-tops and the lovely pale skin above them, as well as the black silk knickers she'd chosen to match her skirt and stockings.

'I've decided to allow you a whisky,' Sarah informed him, 'but not in the way you might expect. I can't have you drinking with me like a free man, that wouldn't do at all,' she said, pouring a little of the whisky onto her panties, just enough to soak them through, 'but perhaps this is a way for a slave to enjoy a whisky with his Mistress. Well?' she added, smiling at his look of amazement. 'What are you waiting for? Don't you want your whisky after I've poured it so carefully for you?'

Barely able to breathe, and sure he must be dreaming, Charles leaned forward and placed his mouth over her whisky soaked panties and began to suck the whisky from them, groaning as he did so, thrilled beyond all sense to drink from her in such a way.

She laughed at his thirsty ardour, and spoke teasingly to inflame him all the more. 'That's the way, Charles, don't miss a drop.'

As he licked and lapped and sucked from her panties, Sarah gave welcome to a secret wetness of her own. 'That feels very nice, I must say,' she said, pouring more whisky over the front of her panties. 'I think it's what you might call killing two birds with one stone.'

Charles drank with even greater ardour, tasting her faintly now through the thin silk of her whisky-soaked panties. Utterly enthralled, he pushed at the wet black silk with his tongue, bringing her the sweetest of pleasures.

'That's lovely, Charles,' she gasped. 'There's some left in the glass. Shall I pour it for you?'

Unable to take his mouth from her, he groaned his assent as he worshipped, and Sarah spoke tenderly, moved by his passion.

'Sweet slave, I'm so glad of you,' she said, pulling her panties to one side, and pouring the rest of the whisky into her forest of dark curls. 'For you, my love. My gift for all your hard work and devotion. Drink from me, Charles, drink from your Mistress.'

Transported by joy, Charles drank from her nakedness, the whisky, now watered by her arousal, tasting of heaven on his adoring tongue.

EVERY DAY on her way to work, Sarah passed by a shop selling costumes and party-wear – fun, trashy stuff such as plastic vampire fangs, viking helmets, monster-masks and dress up costumes for princesses and pirates, maids and witches. But it wasn't the maid's costume that took her eye, it was something far sillier, and even more demeaning. Every time she passed the shop window, she glanced through the glass and told herself she couldn't possibly buy such a thing. It was a preposterous outfit, foolish beyond words, and far too extreme even for her increasingly playful tastes, but it had cast its spell over her, and the day came when she could resist no longer, and she went into the shop and bought the costume. But, when she returned home, she lost her nerve, and hid her purchase at the back of her wardrobe so that Charles wouldn't know of it. A sweet and guilty secret, she liked to think of it in her wardrobe, waiting for the day when she'd find the courage to use it, and she'd often think of the costume, and laugh out loud at the prospect of dressing her slave in it.

Curious about her new sexuality, Sarah had searched the web for sites about dominant women and female-led relationships, astounded by the vast numbers of sites her search unearthed, and both amused and aroused by the stories and images of women taking control of the men in their lives. She wondered why female-led sexuality never received the same public attention or commercial interest as female submission. 'Fifty Shades,' and the many books of its kind that followed, sold in their tens of millions and were discussed openly on radio and television shows, and yet books about men submitting to women remained notable by their absence despite the existence of such classic texts as Sacher-Masoch's 'Venus in Furs,' John Glassco's 'The English Governess,' and Jeanne de Berg's 'Women's Rites,' books that Sarah had read with interest since taking charge of her husband. She found this absence strange as she believed there must be as many men in the world drawn to dominant women as women to dominant men – perhaps an even greater number as it was so much more transgressive and forbidden, and therefore more erotic, at least in her view, for a man to submit to a woman when he is expected by society to be the dominant partner. She could only surmise that patriarchal society had a vested interest in keeping the male longing to submit secret lest it undermined male power in the world, and with it the grinding, profit-driven thrust of capitalism.

Society approved of submissive women, and sought to encourage them, but it wanted nothing to do with submissive men.

Sarah could tell that many of the sites she found were fuelled by male fantasy – she knew that most women wouldn't want to wear tight, restrictive clothing and uncomfortable shoes and underwear, certainly not if they were 'in charge' – and she had little time for those sites. Nor did she think dominant women would have much interest in wielding whips. A truly dominant woman wouldn't need a whip to enforce her authority, the smallest word or look would be enough. Of far more interest to Sarah were the sites that centred on the woman's perspective, and on the fun and freedom a woman could find in a female-led relationship. Quickly able to take a forensic overview of the material, Sarah seldom found the images and stories shocking or pornographic. It came to feel almost natural to look at images of successful women standing proudly above their adoring husbands or lovers, and Sarah soon came to a clear and surprisingly simple understanding – women possessed what men wanted even more than money or status and, in order to win greater freedom, all women had to do was harness their sexual authority, and bring it to bear more openly and honestly in their daily lives. It wouldn't mean the end of romance or love or marriage, far from it – men would be much more enamoured of dominant, sexually confident women than meek housewives – but it might bring about a far healthier balance of power between the sexes. The more Sarah thought about her new lifestyle, the more she understood it wasn't just about sex. She started to see it as a stepping-stone towards a better, fairer, and more feminine world.

One evening she invited Charles to sit beside her on the couch as she was doing one of these searches on her lap-top. 'It seems we're not alone,' she told him, pointing to the huge number of sites found by her search before clicking on the link to an online shop that sold bdsm toys and equipment. 'I thought we should take a look,' said Sarah. 'You never know, we might find something we like. Let me know if you see something that takes your fancy. They're called sex-toys, after all, and we both like to play.'

Charles watched in a state of fearful arousal as Sarah looked at cuffs, and crops and canes, and more extreme items such as male chastity cages, gags and a truly terrifying item of male torture called a humbler. 'My God,' said Sarah, quickly clicking to another item, 'I don't think even I could do that to you. It would put you in hospital, and who'd clean the house then? Who'd wash my knickers and iron my skirts?'

But there was a serious side to Sarah's search. She was eager to try new things, and so she added two sets of leather cuffs with different lengths of chain to her shopping-cart, as well as a matching neck collar and leash. 'I liked it when you put on your ears and were my pussycat for the evening,' she said, 'maybe I'll like it just as much when you're my dog. I'll clip the lead onto your collar, and take you for a walk round the house, maybe into the garden if it's dark. I'll make you walk to heel, Charles, think of that.'

She laughed at his shocked expression, saying, 'Oh, come on, Charles, you'll be a good dog for me, I know you will. A slave needs his shackles, and think how helpless you'll be when I cuff your hands and legs. You won't be able to move unless I let you. I'll be able to do what I like with you, think of that. If I put you somewhere then that's where you'll have to stay until I decide otherwise. Don't look so frightened, it's only a little fun, and I know you'll like it,' she said, chuckling warmly as she scrolled through the items. 'Is there anything else you'd like me to buy? Just say if there is, don't be shy.'

The glimpses of chastity cages and riding-crops, and even the dreadful humbler, had excited Charles greatly, alerting him to the danger of far deeper and more painful forms of surrender, but he dared not admit to his excitement, and so he shook his head, much to Sarah's disappointment.

'That's a shame,' she said. 'I'd hoped you might choose something, and then it wouldn't be all down to me. Go on, pick something, just for me.'

'I don't want to,' he said.

'But I want you to,' said Sarah, 'and it's what I want that counts, you should know that by now. Go on, it'll be our secret.'

Unable to resist her, he pointed blindly to an item on the screen.

'A black rubber bit,' said Sarah, selecting the item, and speaking calmly to hide the excitement she felt at the prospect of robbing him of speech. 'An excellent choice. I'll be able to shut you up whenever I want. What fun we're going to have, but you can pay for them,' she said, passing her lap-top to him. 'You like to buy me gifts, and now's your chance. Buy these for me, Charles, so I can make you even more of a slave.'

Overwhelmed by a delicious drowning feeling, Charles entered his payments details, and placed the order which he was informed would arrive in three weeks time.

'That's three weeks too long if you ask me,' said Sarah, already excited by the thought of using the collar, cuffs and bit on her husband. 'But we'll just have to be patient, won't we? We'll just have to bide our time.'

BUT NOT everything in their lives was about sex. As well as doing all the housework, Charles kept up his search for a new job. He was looking at a very high level, and those positions didn't come up often, but he made his presence felt with emails and calls to past colleagues he thought might be able to help. He called it 'keeping himself in the swim.'

And, now that he had more time on his hands, Sarah asked him to keep in regular contact with their daughters, something he was happy to do. When it came to Kate and Emily, Sarah thought of herself only as a mother and wife, and of Charles as a father and husband. Parenthood was a sacred part of her life, and it took absolute priority over her new relationship with Charles as her slave, and Charles felt exactly the same. Nothing was more important than their children. As far as their daughters were concerned, Sarah and Charles were Mum and Dad, for ever and always, and that was that.

Sarah asked Charles to arrange a short summer holiday with the girls. With Kate in York, and Emily in Edinburgh, it made sense to go North, and Charles booked a week in August in a luxury lodge in The Lake District. 'That's lovely,' Sarah told him. 'We'll go for long walks and have pub-lunches. We'll be an ordinary family again, and take a break from this madness.'

ACM Accountancy, where Sarah had worked for nearly eight years, was a small but successful company that offered financial services to a wide variety of businesses. As Sarah's speciality lay in overseas trade, she was very closely engaged with the confusion and turmoil brought about by Brexit. There was less than a year until the agreed date for the UK to leave the EU, but the rudderless government was no clearer about how leaving would work, and Sarah was acutely aware of the worry this was causing her clients, and she set herself the task of writing a paper outlining the different steps her firm would take to safeguard the interests of their clients according to the very different forms the trade and business outcomes of Brexit might take.

It was a difficult undertaking. She knew the principal aim of the paper must be to reassure her clients, but vague generalisations would be counter-productive, as would pages filled with complex tariff duties and tax-laws. Her first draft was much too long at sixteen pages, and she gave it to Charles, and asked him to help her with it.

He didn't so much rewrite as re-structure it, condensing her four different strategies down to a few punchy paragraphs each, rewording her conclusion as the introduction, and attaching all the detailed rules and figures as appendices. 'That way,' he told her, 'they'll get the gist of the various options very quickly and clearly, and they can look into the details later if they want to. Read it through, and see what you think.'

Sarah did just that, and thought he'd improved it immeasurably. Her paper, now only ten pages long, did exactly what she wanted it to do, offering clarity and reassurance without skating over the complexity of the likely problems to come. 'Thank-you, Charles,' she praised him. 'You've worked wonders.'

'Not at all,' he said. 'You did the hard work.'

'Don't be so modest,' she said, putting down her file, a wicked gleam coming into her eyes. 'Go and fetch the whisky. I think you deserve a nightcap, don't you?'

WHEN THE senior partners read Sarah's paper they decided to circulate it, not only to all their existing clients, but also to new companies in the hope of winning more business, but Sarah's name did not feature on the first draft. Furious at the omission, Sarah strode into Alan Rennie's office and insisted the paper be credited to her. 'It was my idea and my work,' she said firmly. 'It's only right it has my name on it.'

'Of course, Sarah,' Alan quickly agreed. As the Senior Accountant in the firm he'd rather hoped to take the credit himself, and he hadn't expected the quiet and hard-working woman to stand up to him. He'd never seen this side of her before, and he was taken aback by her vehemence. 'Please don't worry, I'll make sure it's done right away.'

'See that you do,' Sarah said, slamming the door on her way out.

'Well done,' Charles said when she told him how she'd put her foot down.

'I should have stood up to him years ago,' she said. 'It's being your Mistress that's done it. I feel so much stronger now, you've no idea. I won't be their dogsbody again, you can be sure of that.'

'I'm glad to hear it,' said Charles, proud of his lovely Mistress, but intimidated by her newfound strength and confidence. He felt as if he was living in a fairy-tale, where he was shrinking inch by inch while his wife was growing taller and stronger with every day that passed.

Growing accustomed to their new relationship, Sarah and Charles lived contentedly as Mistress and slave, finding a serenity in their daily routines that balanced the spice and mischief of their sex-life. But then a number of events, none of them remarkable in their own right, combined to push their marriage into a darker and more precarious place.

Every three months Charles played golf at the famous Wentworth course, and the date for the next round was fast approaching, but he wasn't sure he wanted to play. His friends George Durrell and David Schama would be there, and he looked forward to seeing them, and he loved the course, but Ryan Moore had been his partner the last two times they played, and he was due to play again this time. Charles still carried a burning anger towards his ex-friend and assistant, and he had no desire to see him.

'Of course you should go,' Sarah told him when he talked to her about it. 'David and George are your friends. Why should you miss out on seeing them just because of a pushy bastard like Ryan Moore? And rounds at Wentworth are rarer than gold. No, Charles, you must go. In fact, I insist on it. Enjoy yourself, show David and George you couldn't care less about Ryan. Rise above it, show them you're too big a man to carry stupid grudges. It'll be good for you, I know it will. It'll help you put it behind you once and for all.'

But Charles didn't enjoy himself. He put on a brave and cheerful front, but he found the whole day to be an ordeal. Apart from anything else he played terrible golf while Ryan played well above his usual standard. Charles should have been pleased about this as Ryan was his partner, and his excellent play won them the match on the final hole, but Charles took no joy in their victory and afterwards, while they ate a delicious meal in the clubhouse, he felt hurt to see how well David and George got on with his rival. He could see that they looked up to Ryan, and viewed him as the coming man. Ryan never mentioned work but everything about him radiated strength and success, and Charles couldn't help but feel defeated by him all over again.

But this time the pain of defeat felt different. This time, to his confusion, it felt oddly pleasurable.

'Well, how was it?' Sarah asked him when he got back.

'I'm glad it's over, to tell the truth,' he said wearily.

'How were David and George?'

'Very well, as far as I could tell.'

'And did Ryan behave himself?' she asked, more interested than she should have been, and oddly aroused to see Charles so pale and tired.

'On the face of it,' said Charles, 'but he was having the time of his life – lording it, telling jokes and going on about his new apartment, making sure we all knew how well he was doing. It was pathetic really, and you should have seen him in the shower-room, laughing and drying his dick in front of everyone like he's king of the world. God knows why I ever thought of him as a friend.'

'Never mind, you're home now,' said Sarah, shaken by how much Charles' description of Ryan had excited her. For some reason she took pleasure in Ryan's ascendancy over her husband, and thinking of him lording it over his vanquished rivals, far from seeming pathetic, woke in her a dark and primitive arousal. It was a silly and immature response, she knew that perfectly well, but all the same she couldn't stop thinking of Ryan showing off in the shower-room. It made him seem masterful and alluring. That night she let Charles make love to her, but it was Ryan's arrogant smile and tall, rangy body that filled her mind.

He was victor ludorum, and she was his prize.

After spending six weeks waiting for a new CEO position to come up, two came up in as many days, and Charles polished his impressive resumé and applied for both posts. Sarah had conflicted feelings about this. Of course she wanted her husband to succeed and get back to work – or so she told herself – but another part of her loved her new life as a Mistress, and didn't want to lose the services of her besotted and adoring slave.

Charles was disappointed not to be interviewed for his preferred job, and then he read that the company had recently developed strong links with Joseph & Hill, Charles' most recent employers.

'That bastard Ryan Moore,' he told Sarah. 'He'll have blocked me, you can be sure of it.'

'You don't know that,' said Sarah.

'It's how he works,' said Charles. 'Once he's got you down he likes to keep you there.'

'Just like me,' Sarah thought, experiencing a jolt of arousal that brought colour to her cheeks, and made her look away to hide her excitement.

But Charles was invited to interview for the second post, and he received a friendly call from Julie Carrington, the current CEO whom both Charles and Sarah knew and liked. 'I'm looking to step back, and retire in a year or so,' she told Charles. 'I think you'll be a perfect fit to take over, and I'm delighted that you're interested.'

Charles' interview was arranged for five days time, and Sarah resigned herself to losing her slave, but then she encountered Julie entirely by chance at a trade convention, and did something terrible. She hadn't planned to do it. It just happened, like an accident she didn't see coming.

'Can I have a quick word?' she asked Julie during a break in the morning session.

'Of course you can,' said Julie, pouring coffee, and leading Sarah to a quiet corner of the conference room.

'I'm way out of line here,' said Sarah, her heart pounding, 'and I want to apologise for that in advance.'

'What is it?' said Julie.

'I know you're seeing Charles for the CEO position.'

'I am,' said Julie, 'but I would have expected him to tell you about that.'

'I know, but I don't think he's ready to go back to work.'

'In what way?' said Julie, frowning with worry.

'I shouldn't say this,' said Sarah, astonished at her behaviour. 'It's a dreadful breach of confidence, I know that, but Charles had been suffering from stress before he left Joseph and Hill, and he's been so much better for being at home. It's doing him the world of good to take a break from work.'

'He sounded fine on the phone,' said Julie.

'Oh, he won't admit to anything,' said Sarah. 'As far as Charles is concerned stress and depression don't exist, you know what men are like.'

'Indeed I do,' said Julie, nodding her head gravely.

Sarah had heard rumours that Julie's husband had taken extended breaks from work due to stress and anxiety, and she was banking on this influencing her view of Charles.

'I'm only saying this because I'm worried about his health,' said Sarah.

'It's a shame,' said Julie. 'He'd be great for us.'

'He would,' said Sarah. 'He'd do a wonderful job. Oh, now I wish I'd never said anything.'

'Don't be silly,' said Julie. 'Your husband's health comes before everything.'

'Thank-you, Julie,' said Sarah. 'But please keep this between the two of us. Charles would be furious if he knew I'd spoken to you.'

'Of course, but I'll have to go through with the interview. It would look strange if I cancelled at this late date.'

'Poor Charles,' said Sarah. 'He likes you, and he's so excited about the job. I'm sure he'll give a great interview.'

'I'll do what's right,' said Julie, 'and I'm very glad you told me.'

After their talk, horrified by what she'd done, yet exhilarated by her betrayal, Sarah went straight to the ladies' room. Alone in the cubicle she leaned her forehead against the coolness of the wall and waited for her breathing to slow and her racing heart to steady. What had she done? Had she really just betrayed her husband and plotted his failure so she could keep him at home as her slave? Had she put her own selfish pleasure above his happiness and success? She couldn't have, not Sarah Hunter, not the loving and supportive wife, not the honest and forthright woman who always put husband and family first. But her breathing didn't slow, and her heart didn't steady. On the contrary, her excitement only grew stronger until, driven by an arousal she could neither understand nor control, she reached under her skirt and pleasured herself, coming quickly and with such force she had to bite her lip to stop herself from crying out.

This dark and unsettling excitement stayed with Sarah over the next few days as she helped Charles prepare for his interview. She noticed how he'd become much less submissive now he expected to escape from his servitude, and Sarah went along with that, playing her role as his loyal wife, knowing she'd soon have him in her power again. She helped him choose a new suit for his interview, agreeing that he must wear boxer shorts under it. 'I want you to win,' she told him, astonished by her duplicity, and the pleasure she found in it. 'And winners don't wear panties.'

She even went over his presentation with him, making suggestions as to how he could improve it. Her behaviour troubled her, and gave her an entirely new perspective on her life and character. Plagued by guilt, she stepped back from herself, disgusted at what she'd done, and seeing herself, not as a real person, but as a character in a book or film – a Mata-Hari, a femme fatale, a woman without conscience, a spy in the house of love. She thought it an accurate enough view of the woman she'd become. Wasn't she using sex and cunning to get what she wanted? Hadn't she stepped beyond the bounds of morality, and committed an unforgivable crime against the partner in her life? She could only answer in the affirmative, the realisation bringing her a thrill of fear. Women in books and films who behaved as she had invariably paid for their sins, and she took some comfort in the fact that she'd soon be judged and punished.

And yet Sarah found pleasure in her sin and guilt. She didn't see herself as dull any more, as an ordinary woman leading an ordinary life. She was an outlaw now, a rebel who'd broken the rules, and backed a dark and selfish instinct she knew she should have suppressed but, rather than being brought low by her crime, her brain felt sharper, and her nerve-ends alive with excitement. Whatever crime she'd committed, she had no option but to see it through, and accept what pain or pleasure resulted from her actions.

On the morning of Charles' interview Sarah was his loving wife and companion, pressing his shirt and helping him chose his tie, before cooking breakfast for him. His interview wasn't until ten thirty, and she had to leave before him, but she told him how handsome he looked in his new suit, and she kissed him, and wished him luck. It aroused her to see how hopeful he looked.

She passed the party shop on her way to work and thought of the costume hidden in her wardrobe. She couldn't make Charles wear it, could she? It would be inexcusably cruel, and yet she couldn't get the idea out of her head. Her moral compass had lost its bearings for the unforgivable cruelty of the idea somehow only made it more appealing. All morning she couldn't shake off a peculiar feeling of guilt mixed with excitement. She knew she should feel terrible about what she'd done, and yet an elusive arousal danced in her blood. If she could so selfishly sabotage her husband's life, what else might she be capable of? What else might she do to her poor, unsuspecting husband?

'You'd better be careful, dear husband,' she thought darkly on her way to the ladies' room. 'Very, very careful.'

She waited until twelve before calling him, but his phone was switched off. She tried again at just before one, and this time he answered.

'Where are you?' she asked him, hearing the sound of traffic.

'I'm on my way home,' he said.

'How did it go?'

'Hard to say,' he said, sounding flat. 'Fine, I suppose, but something didn't feel right. Julie was friendly enough, as were the other two on the interview panel, and my presentation went down well, but Julie seemed distracted and remote. I can't put my finger on it, but something felt wrong.'

'You're imagining it,' Sarah said, her stomach fluttering with excitement. 'It'll be fine, I'm sure.'

'Let's hope so,' said Charles. 'It's a great job, and I know I'm right for it.'

'I'm sure you are, and I'm sure Julie feels the same.'

'Well, fingers crossed,' he said, suddenly sounding wrung-out, and very weary.

'I'll see you tonight,' she said, pushing away her guilt.

'Love you,' he said.

'Love you too,' said Sarah.

'Sarah, before you go?'

'What is it?' she said, worried he suspected something.

'Thank-you for everything,' he said. 'For all your help and support and for … you know what. I don't know how I'd get by without you.'

'You're very welcome.'

'I think the world of you,' he said before ending the call.

Going back to her desk, Sarah was surprised to discover she felt almost entirely free of guilt, and she recalled a Patricia Highsmith novel she'd read many years ago. She'd loved the clarity and toughness of the writing, but she hadn't believed the main character's complete lack of a moral conscience. People just weren't like that, she'd felt at the time.

But now she wasn't so sure.

She didn't ring the doorbell when she got home. She sensed the time wasn't right to take up the reins in her marriage again. Charles would still be in limbo after his interview, one part free man, the other slave, and she was happy to let events unfold at their own pace. Startled by Sarah's unannounced arrival, Charles jumped to his feet and helped her off with her coat, asking if she'd like a cup of tea.

'No, I'll make you one,' she said, filling the kettle. 'But tell me, have you heard anything?'

'Still nothing,' he said. 'Not a good sign.'

'You don't know that.'

'I think I do. I've interviewed enough people to know that when you want someone you usually let them know the same day.'

'There's still time,' said Sarah, glancing at her watch.

As if agreeing with her, Charles' phone rang. He took it from his pocket and glanced at its screen.

'It's Julie,' he said, hurrying out to the hallway where he could take the call in private.

While he talked, Sarah paced up and down, seized by excitement and the anticipation of success. His call lasted for several minutes, long enough for her to fear that Julie had given him the job after all, but when he came back into the kitchen he looked so pale and dejected Sarah knew her plan had worked.

'Oh, Charles, I'm so sorry,' she said, hugging him.

'I can't understand it,' he said. 'Everything looked so good, but now Julie's decided not to step back for another year or more, and suddenly there's no vacancy.'

'What did she say?'

'Oh, she kept apologising for wasting my time, and said it was no reflection on my qualities, and that maybe in a year or two she'll think again.'

'You'll get over it.'

'I'm not sure I will,' he said. 'This one hurts. I don't know why but it's got right through my defences. I feel crushed by it, really I do. I was so sure it was going to work out, and now I don't know what to do with myself, honestly, Sarah, I don't.'

'But I know what to do with you,' she said. 'I'm taking you out for a meal. Come on, no more brooding. You look so handsome in your suit, I want to show you off to the world.'

'I don't feel like it.'

'Too bad, we're going.'

They walked to Gigi's, Charles' favourite Italian restaurant where Sarah plied him with food and wine until his mood improved enough for her to begin weaving her spell again.

'I'm sorry today didn't go as you wanted,' she said, touching the toe of her shoe against his ankle, 'but it's not all bad news, is it? In fact, if I'm honest, I'm really quite pleased you're not going back to work.'

'What do you mean?'

'You know what I mean.'

'Not now,' he said, looking around nervously. 'Not here.'

'Why not?'

'People will hear,' Charles said in a loud whisper.

'Then I'll speak quietly,' said Sarah leaning across the table, putting her hand on Charles' hand, and speaking in a warm whisper. 'Now you're not going back to work, things can stay as they are. I can go on being your Mistress, and you can go on being my slave. That's good news, don't you think? Maybe we should be celebrating instead of drowning our sorrows.'

'Jesus, Sarah,' said Charles. 'You can't see it like that.'

'I can see it any way I like.'

'We can't keep living that way, it's not possible.'

'Why not, it's fun, isn't it?'

'It's too much fun,' he said, a grave expression on his handsome face. 'It scares me how much I like it. That's why I wanted this job so badly, so I could go back to leading a normal life again, because if I don't … '

He fell silent, unable to find the words.

'If you don't, what?' said Sarah, still rubbing her shoe against his leg.

'If I don't stop, it'll take over my life.'

'Is that such a bad thing?'

'You know it is.'

'Do I?' she said. 'All I know is how happy we've been these past six weeks, happier than an old married couple like us have any right to be. Do you deny it?'

'No, but ...'

'Why does there have to be a but?'

'It's too strong,' said Charles. 'It's like a drug, I want more and more until ... God knows what ... Until I can't live without it.'

'Some people might say you've just described love,' said Sarah, signalling to the waiter to bring Charles another brandy.

'If it's love then it's a very dangerous kind.'

'Isn't that the best kind?'

'It comes at a cost, Sarah, believe me.'

'What cost?'

'Isn't that obvious? Pride, self-respect, the ability to function normally in the world.'

'Oh, come on,' said Sarah, her eyes sparkling. 'You function very well as my slave, can't you take pride in that?'

'Be serious.'

'I am being serious. We've found the courage to have a different kind of marriage, and we should be proud of that.'

'That's fine for you,' he answered, wishing she'd see it more from his side. 'Your life goes on as normal – you go to work, meet your friends, dress as you want – but think what it's like for me, trapped at home, living as your slave. You once said it was a kind of magic. Well if it is, it's dark magic. It's not healthy, Sarah, can't you see that? There's a sickness in it, a pleasure so ripe it's on the point of rotting. Pleasure that strong can't exist without doing damage, without exacting a toll.'

'Maybe it's a price worth paying.'

'I'm not sure it is.'

They waited in silence for a few moments while the waiter brought Charles his brandy.

'Or maybe we've been conditioned to be afraid of pleasure,' Sarah continued once the waiter had gone, 'and stay in our little boxes like rats in a trap. Maybe we have a much greater capacity for sexual pleasure than society allows us. And maybe with that pleasure comes creativity, freedom, the ability to think for ourselves, the chance to make a better world.'

'Or it's an excuse to fiddle while Rome burns, and indulge our darker instincts.'

'That's the risk we take.'

'We don't have to take the risk. We could stop, take a break at least.'

'Yes, but I don't want to.'

'Come on, Sarah, do you really think it's an acceptable way to live?'

'I don't see why not,' said Sarah. 'And who decides what's acceptable and what's not? I don't understand it any more than you do, but I feel better for having some danger in my life, something wild and new. It is scary, of course it is, but I like being scared. I like being able to play, and not know how the game will turn out. If you're honest, I think you do too.'

'Sometimes I think you're a witch,' said Charles, captivated by her spark and beauty. 'Honestly, I do.'

'Oh dear, you've guessed my secret,' said Sarah, laughing as she spoke, yet a part of her believing sex really had given her new powers. 'Take care, Charles, or I'll turn you into my cat, or one of my slips, and I'll wear you all day long under my silkiest dress. If I'm feeling kind, I may even wear you to bed.'

Aroused by her playfulness, he blushed and looked away, but Sarah just laughed, and said, 'You'd like that wouldn't you?'

'I like everything you do.'

'Then why stop?'

'Because it frightens me.'

'I've told you, that's part of it. It wouldn't be so much fun if it wasn't frightening.'

'I never dreamed you could be like this,' he said, truly fearful of her.

'Neither did I,' said Sarah, squeezing his hand, and looking into his eyes. 'And there's so much more we can do, so much more fun we can have. Don't you want to experience all that?'

'Throw away the map?'

'Yes.'

'You mean it, don't you?'

'Yes, I believe I do.'

'But where does it go? How does it end?'

'Where does anything go? How does anything end?'

'I'm not as brave as you.'

'You're not a coward, I know that.'

'Go easy,' said Charles. 'After today I'm feeling a little fragile to say the least.'

'You mean you might break?'

'I think I might.'

'So much the better,' she said with a wicked smile.

Charles drank his brandy and looked at his wife, truly fearful of her, and yet thrilled by her wit and natural authority. He could no longer see her as an ordinary woman. Everything about her seemed enchanting and dangerous, and infinitely alluring, and a part of him longed to give over his life entirely to her pleasure and happiness.

On their walk home Sarah clung to his arm, and leaned her head against his shoulder, giving them the appearance of strolling lovers, but the words she spoke to him were hardly romantic, at least not in any conventional way.

'When we get home,' she told him, 'I'm going to be your Mistress again, and you'll be my slave. You'll take my coat and kneel at my feet the way you do when I come home from work. Is that understood?'

'Yes,' he said meekly, once more under her spell.

'I'm going to be cruel to you tonight,' she said. 'But you'll feel better for it, I know you will.'

Overwhelmed with love for her, Charles took her in his arms and crushed her lips to his in a never-ending embrace. It was a heavenly kiss that left them as dizzy and transported as young lovers.

When they got inside Sarah experienced a sweet thrill of power when he took her coat before kneeling to kiss the hem of her skirt, and her lovely, nylon-clad knees.

'That's what a woman likes,' she said, ruffling his thick, sandy hair. 'A man on his knees.' And then, pulling him to his feet, she looked into his eyes as she undid his belt and took down his trousers. 'Here's the problem,' she said, caressing him through his boxer shorts. 'Wearing these silly things as if you're a proper man. You're much happier in panties, of course you are. It's not good for you to pretend you're a real man, it makes you confused and unhappy. Go upstairs, Charles. You'll find a pair of my knickers in the laundry basket. As I remember, they're quite a pretty pair. Put them on and get into bed. I'll be up in a little while. On you go, now,' she said, smiling as she watched him climb the stairs to their bedroom with a slow, heavy tread. 'I won't be long.'

Once he'd undressed Charles went naked into the shower-room where he experienced a masochistic arousal far deeper and more overwhelming than any he'd felt before. Failure to find work had undermined his already fragile confidence, and left him even more vulnerable to his sickly appetites. Reaching into the laundry basket, he found her knickers, a pretty white pair embroidered with tiny yellow flowers. He hesitated before putting them on, fearing that wearing them would mark another step in his descent towards complete surrender and that, if he wasn't careful, he'd become her slave forever. He tried to think clearly, and remember the man he used to be, but his brain was in a fog and he couldn't resist the lure of Sarah's authority. His hands shaking, his cock growing submissively erect, he stepped into the panties, and pulled them up his legs.

He got quickly into bed as if to hide his shame from the world. But there was no hiding. As he lay waiting for his Mistress, shame overwhelmed him and brought with it an excitement so great he truly believed he was awaiting the arrival, not of his wife, but of a goddess, a female spirit of light and darkness.

It was over forty minutes before Sarah finally came upstairs. She knew making Charles wait would increase his anticipation, and she sensed his excitement as soon as she came into the bedroom. In the soft light from the bedside lamp, the wonder in his eyes made her think of a small boy on Christmas Eve who'd seen Santa Claus at last.

'Sorry to be so long,' Sarah said, sitting on the bed beside him, and leaning down to kiss his forehead so he could smell her perfume and feel her soft hair brush against his face. 'I've been on my lap-top, looking to buy you a gift.'

She hadn't been doing any such thing – she'd been texting her friends Louise and Rebecca to arrange a night-out – but she wanted Charles to believe she'd been shopping online. It was part of the story she planned to tell him.

'You've had such a hard day,' she said kindly, 'I wanted to buy you something to make up for it. Do you want to know what it is, or would you rather it's a surprise?'

'I d-don't know,' he said, happy just to be in the presence of his Goddess.

'I'm going to tell you,' she said. 'I've been looking for a maid's uniform. I know how much you like it when I make you dress as a maid in my stories, and it's high time I dress you as my maid in real life. Then it won't just be a story any more. You're going to have your very own maid's uniform, Charles. I'll even teach you to curtsey. Won't that be fun?'

Charles' eyes grew wider, making Sarah laugh, but he remained silent. He didn't trust himself to speak.

'I don't like the uniforms you find on sex-sites – they're too silly and make-believe. No, I want you in a proper maid's uniform, the kind of uniform a real maid might wear when she's working in a hotel or serving in a restaurant – something neat and practical – and so I started searching hospitality and catering workwear sites.'

This part was true, although she'd carried out the search several days ago, when Charles was preparing for his interview.

'Good news,' she continued. 'I've found several that will do perfectly. They even have ladies' shoes in wider fittings with one and a half inch heels – not too high for you but neat and pretty all the same. I haven't placed an order yet because I need to take your measurements, and I thought you'd like to help me choose, but we'll do that soon, Charles, I promise, very soon.'

Smiling with satisfaction, Sarah took off one of her shoes. It made a soft shucking sound, and Sarah saw Charles look at her shoe with hunger in his eyes.

'Do you like my shoe?' she asked him, not waiting for an answer. 'It's the same one I touched your leg with in the restaurant tonight under the table,

I'm sure you remember.' Holding her shoe to his mouth, she said, 'Kiss it, Charles. Kiss my pretty shoe.'

Utterly bewitched, Charles' eyes closed in delight as he kissed the smooth leather of the little high-heeled shoe.

'That's what I like to see,' said Sarah. 'A grateful and obedient slave. Perhaps you'd like to smell it too. Oh yes, I'm sure you'll like that.'

Smiling down at him, she placed the opening of her shoe over his mouth and nose, and held it there.

'Look at you,' she said, a smile in her voice. 'Lying there with my shoe over your face. If you'll take this from me, there's no knowing what else you'll take.'

He made a soft, moaning sound, and breathed in more deeply.

'That's it, deep breaths,' she said, a nurse giving oxygen to her patient. 'I've been wearing it all day, but I know how much you like my different smells.'

She kept him like that for long moments, laughing as he breathed in the scent of her sweaty tights and worn shoe leather, and then she stood and took the shoe away from him, pleased by the lost, dreamy look it had brought to his eyes. She put on a show for him as she undressed, slowly unbuttoning her blouse before taking it off, then unzipping her skirt and stepping out of it so that she stood by the bed in just her slip. Reaching behind her, she unclipped her bra, disentangling it from the straps of her slip, and allowing him a glimpse of her lovely, full breasts before covering them again with the lace of her slip. Then she reached beneath her slip, tugging down her hose and panties and dangling them against Charles' face, tormenting him with their wispy allure.

'There,' she taunted him. 'What you like best of all – my dirty nylons and panties. Well, Charles, what do you say?'

'Th-thank-you,' he gasped.

'I beg your pardon.'

'Thank-you, Mistress.'

'You're very welcome,' she said, dropping her panties and hose onto his face, and getting into bed.

She lay close against him, her head on his shoulder and her hand on his erection that was pushing beyond the waistband of her knickers as if striving to prove how manly he was.

'I love you like this,' she said. 'All hard in your panties, but winners don't wear panties, do they? I told you that when we were shopping for your suit.'

He gave a groan, his cock pulsing in her hand.

'If winners don't wear panties,' she said cruelly, loosening her grip a little to stop him from coming, 'then what kind of men do wear panties?'

He gave another groan, and said nothing.

'Answer me, Charles,' she said. 'It's not difficult. What kind of men wear panties?'

'Losers,' he gasped.

'That's right,' she said approvingly, pleased with her pupil. 'And what must that make you?'

'Please ...' he begged her, not wanting to answer.

'Come on,' she said, taking her hand from his cock and pushing her worn panties and hose harder against his nose. 'How many times have I spoken to you about telling the truth? I'll ask you again – what must that make you?'

'A l-loser,' he stammered, a wave of masochistic arousal washing through him.

'That's right,' she agreed, 'and that's why I'm going to dress you as my maid, so the whole world can see what a loser you are. It'll be for the best in the long run. Once you're in uniform no-one will make the mistake of thinking you're a real man. You won't have to pretend any more. In a strange kind of way, you'll be free. You may not believe it, but it will be an act of the greatest love and kindness.'

He gave a long sigh, and Sarah knew he was falling into the trance her bed-time stories always provoked in him, and she began to tell the story he never tired of hearing – the story of the party she'd hold with him serving as her uniformed maid. It was a fantasy that captivated Charles like no other, and it had reached the point where he wanted to hear it every night, such was the delight he took in imagining his public degradation. If she was feeling particularly cruel, she'd make him beg her to tell it.

'Not that silly story again,' she'd say, contempt in her voice.

'Please, Mistress,' he'd say in a frenzy of need.

'I'm not in the mood.'

'Please.'

'Only a fool wants to hear the same thing again and again.'

'Then I'm a fool,' he'd reply. 'Forgive me, but I am.'

'I'm bored with you, and I'm bored with telling you the same old story.'

'Please, Mistress,' he'd beseech her, a starving man begging for food. 'Tell me again about your party, and the uniform you'll make me wear. Tell me how frightened I'll be before the guests arrive. Tell me how you'll only laugh at my fear. Tell me about the party-dress you'll wear, and how lovely you'll look while I'm serving as your maid. Tell me about your underwear, and the new shoes and stockings you've bought for the party. Tell me how I'll help you get dressed for the party. Tell me how I'll look out your underwear and kneel at your feet to help you on with your shoes. Tell me what perfume you'll wear, and how you'll style your hair. Tell me how you'll make me answer the door to your guests. Tell me how I'll have to curtsey. Tell me how you'll slap me if I start to cry. Tell me how you'll laugh and dance and drink with other men and never pay me the slightest attention. Tell me how everyone will laugh at me in my dress and apron. Tell me how your laugh will be the loudest of all. Tell me, Mistress, please, I beg you.'

By now Charles could tell himself the story, the repetition and ritual of it only making the story more erotic for him, a fantasia of the deepest pain and humiliation, but he needed to hear it from Sarah. Her warm, mocking voice thrilled him to the core, and carried him off to the cruellest heaven. But, in truth, Sarah had grown weary of telling him the same old story, regardless of how deeply the repetition enslaved her husband – and this night she decided to add new details to sharpen her interest, and deepen his humiliation, and lead them closer to the dark heart of the forest.

'I've told you of being a serving-maid at my party many time before,' Sarah said, 'but I've never really spoken of the guest-list, at least not in any detail.'

She settled into her customary position with her head on his shoulder, whispering in his ear as he breathed in the intoxicating scent from her panties, and cupping his balls through the knickers he was wearing while he stroked himself lightly, looking to prolong his pleasure for as long as he could.

'This will be a special party,' she informed him, 'with some new and very special guests. You'll be wearing your best uniform in their honour, and you'll look very smart in your little black dress and white apron, and neat black shoes – very attentive and ready to serve – but this time you'll be wearing a full petticoat under your dress, and we'll have the pleasure of seeing it every time you curtsey, like snow falling on a dark and frosty night.'

He groaned softly, very aroused by the addition of the petticoats under his uniform, and by the lovely way she described it. He muttered something dreamily under his breath that sounded like 'Help me.'

But there was no help to be had.

'Now, Charles, I want you to imagine the party's in full swing,' said Sarah in a slow, husky murmur. 'All your old colleagues from work will be there, and all our friends and family too.

'No,' he gasped, but Sarah felt him tense as his arousal deepened.

'Of course they'll be there. This is the party where everything comes out into the open once and for all, and I'll have sent out invitations far and wide. Even your sister will be there, all the way from Italy.'

Charles winced and cried out as if she'd punched him, but Sarah knew the effect mentioning his sister would have. Charles had always been very competitive with his older sister, and always wanted her to think highly of him.

'Francesca has to be there,' Sarah continued. 'You know how she's always wanted to get the better of you, and I'm sure she'll love to see how I've turned you into my pretty little maid. Perhaps I'll get her to design you a new uniform.'

Francesca was a highly successful fashion designer in Rome, and Sarah smiled to think of the crisply elegant maid's uniform Francesca might design for her little brother.

But there was something else that excited Sarah about Francesca coming to the party. Like Charles' parents, Francesca had always looked down on Sarah, thinking her common and dull. It would be wonderful to show her that she was far stronger and more interesting than she'd imagined. It would be lovely to show her that she, and not her wealthy, privileged brother, had taken charge of their marriage, and the fact that Francesca would find pleasure in her brother's downfall only added to Sarah's pleasure.

'And besides,' said Sarah, 'I'm tired of hiding and keeping secrets. I want everyone to know you're my slave, and no longer my husband. Everyone will be there, Charles, I promise you. Some will be shocked, I suppose, and some will laugh at you, but they'll soon get used to you serving drinks and passing round food. And you know what people are like. Deep down, they'll love seeing the great Charles Hunter dressed as his wife's maid. "How have the mighty fallen," they'll whisper to each other as you go past in your little dress, your hands shaking, and your face red with shame. They'll laugh and talk about it long after the party's over.'

'Oh, God,' he mumbled. 'Oh, God.'

'If anyone asks, I'll say you've suffered a breakdown and can only live as my slave and maid. I'll tell them the big bad world has become too much for you, and you have to hide away from it. I'll tell them you can't make decisions for yourself any more, and I have to make them for you. The funny thing is, Charles, they'll feel sorry for me, tell me how kind and understanding I am to put up with you.'

He made a sound like a sob, but Sarah felt his body tremble with excitement.

'And then the doorbell will ring,' she continued. 'Another of my special guests will have arrived, and I'll send you to answer the door. Can you guess who it will be?'

'No,' he gasped in an agony of dread.

'It'll be Julie Carrington.'

'No,' he protested, appalled yet deeply thrilled.

'Yes,' Sarah insisted. 'I want her to see what you're really like. How glad she'll be then she didn't give you the job. "If I'd known he was like this," she'll say to me once we've hugged and kissed, "I would never have interviewed him. Thank goodness I didn't appoint him. But he looks so good in his uniform, and he curtsies so nicely, I'm sure it's for the best."'

'"Oh, it is for the best," I'll reply. "He's much happier living as a maid. He won't be going back to his old work, not now he's discovered his real self. This is how he'll live from now on, as my maid and housekeeper. His days of going out to work, of being the big man, are long gone."'

Charles gave a groan of defeat as if some engine deep inside him had wound down and ceased its struggle, and Sarah, sensing his capitulation, felt a surge of raw female power. As she'd hoped, bringing the real disappointment of his interview into her story greatly strengthened the erotic impact of her tale. It made her story feel true to him, and his submission real and inescapable. It also wove her own betrayal secretly into the story in a way that greatly heightened her own excitement, and allowed her to enjoy the fruits of her cruelty.

But Sarah had another torment in store for him, a torment so dark and devilish she wondered it she dared say it.

'But I've invited another guest to my party,' she whispered, risking all. 'A very special guest.'

He moaned, and shook his head as if he couldn't take any more.

But he could take more. She was going to make him.

'Don't you want to know who it is?' she asked him.

'N-no,' he stammered weakly.

'Oh, I think you do. Shall I tell you?'

'Please, no,' he gasped.

'Actually, I'm not sure I should tell you,' she said. 'It will hurt so much it might make you cry, and that would be a pity. But I suppose it's alright for a slave to cry. Slaves have given up their pride, haven't they? They don't have to be strong like real men are strong. No-one minds when a slave cries, and so I'm going to tell you, Charles, I'm going to tell you the name of my special guest even if it makes you cry. Are you ready to hear?'

Once more he shook his head from side to side, quicker this time, in a frenzy of anxiety, but Sarah felt his body quiver with excitement, and stretch up in an arc so that only his heels and the back of his head still touched the bed.

'I warn you, Charles, it's someone you hate,' she whispered so that he moaned with fear and arousal. 'Someone you hate very much, but it's funny how this works, isn't it? For all your hatred, I think it's who you most want to come to my party. It's who you most want to answer the door to, it's who you most want to be seen by in your little maid's dress and petticoats. Oh, yes, Charles, I think it is, and when the doorbell rings, I think you'll know deep in your heart exactly who it will be.'

'Help me,' he sobbed from a place beyond pride.

'There is no help,' Sarah said, fascinated by the depth of his trance. 'And when the doorbell rings, I'll tell you to hurry up and answer it. You'll know from the smile in my eyes who my guest is, but I won't spare you. I'll be having too much fun. "And don't forget to curtsey," I'll tell you as you go to answer the door. And you will go to the door in your little dress and apron, your pretty shoes click-clacking on the hall tiles, and your hand shaking as you take hold of the handle, but you'll open the door, Charles, truly you will … And there he'll be.'

'Please,' he gasped. 'Not him.'

'Yes,' said Sarah. 'Ryan Moore.'

Charles howled at the sound of the name as if he'd been struck by an arrow through the heart, and he began to buck and thrash as if he was having a fit.

'Easy, now,' Sarah said in the voice she might use to a frightened horse, pushing down on him and holding her worn panties tighter against his nose. 'Of course Ryan will come. I want everyone to see how we live and what you've become. Then we won't need to pretend any more, and we can live openly as Mistress and slave. Of course Ryan will laugh at you in your uniform – how could he not? – and he'll love it when you curtsey to him. "Don't cry," he'll say when he sees the tears in your eyes. "You look very pretty in your dress, and I always knew you were a slave."'

'"Dry your tears, Charles," I'll say, "and bring Ryan a drink," but when you come back with his drink I'll be dancing with him, dancing and laughing. Well, why shouldn't I? After all, he's a handsome, successful man, and women are very attracted to men like that. You'll just have to stand and watch me dance with him. And everyone at the party will see us dancing. How they'll pity you, and laugh at you to see your wife dancing with your greatest rival. I know that's cruel of me, Charles, but Mistresses can be cruel sometimes, I'm afraid that's just the way of the world.'

Charles moaned as if in pain, and another tremor wracked his body, but his hand moved faster on his erection and Sarah knew a deeper, darker addiction had taken root in him, that he'd moved from soft to hard drugs. And Sarah felt it too, the thought of dancing with Ryan in front of her husband waking a wild streak in her, and making her want to heap coals on the flames of Charles' torment.

'I'll like dancing with him,' she whispered, her mouth so close he could feel her breath on his cheek. 'He's such a tall, handsome man with those broad shoulders and long legs and that shining black hair. Oh, yes, I'll like dancing with him very much, particularly when a slow song begins to play and we can hold each other close.'

Charles made another sobbing sound, and Sarah moved her hand alongside his, her fingers fluttering around his erection. 'Sssh, it's alright,' she whispered. 'You're allowed to like it. I want you to like it. You're only a slave and a slave has no say in what happens, none at all. Give up, Charles. Give up and accept your fate. This had to happen, you know it did.'

'It hurts,' he moaned. 'It hurts so much.'

She noticed that tears glistened on his cheeks even as his erection filled her hand, but she felt little pity for him. On the contrary, her arousal only grew stronger.

'I know,' she said gently, the faint pity she felt for him sweetening her joy, 'but you like me to hurt you. You like it more than anything else in the world. That's why I invited Ryan, because I knew how much it would hurt you.'

'Oh, God,' he gasped.

'I'm a cruel woman, that's why you love me.'

He lifted his head from the pillow and threw it back again, his eyes clenched shut, and his breath coming in short gasps.

'I could hurt you even more?' she said, gripping him tighter, but letting go when she felt him pulse in her hand. She didn't want him to come, at least not yet. She was enjoying herself too much. 'Should I, Charles, should I be bad to you? I can be very bad if you want. Just say if you'd like that. I can be good or I can be bad. Tell me which one you want.'

Caught between heaven and hell, he made a strange, choking sound.

'I didn't hear you,' she said.

'B-bad,' he stammered.

'You want me to be bad?'

'Y-yes.'

'Very bad?'

'Yes.'

'Beg me,' she said, thrilled by her ridiculous game, and the very real power it gave her.

'I beg you,' he gasped.

'You're begging me to hurt you?'

'Yes, I'm begging you,' he said, his voice weak and tremulous.

'Louder, Charles. I want to hear you say it loud and clear.'

'Hurt me,' he begged her. 'Please, I beg you. I'm a slave, do what you like with me.'

'Even if it hurts very much?'

'Yes.'

'More than you can bear?'

'Yes.'

'Even if it makes you cry?'

'Yes,' he beseeched her. 'Make me cry, please, I beg you.'

'Oh, I will, believe me,' Sarah said in his ear, returning eagerly to her story. 'We'll be slow-dancing, Ryan and I, and you'll be watching us from a corner with tears running down your face, and all the guests will be watching you to see what you do. But you won't do anything, will you, Charles? You're just the maid, and there's nothing a maid can do, not against a big, strong man like Ryan Moore. If you tried to stop him he'd just put you over his knee, pull up your petticoats and spank you in front of everyone. Then you'd really have something to cry about. And I wouldn't stop him. Oh, no, I'd just laugh along with everyone else. "Harder," I'd shout. "Hurt him. Teach him his place. Make sure he learns his lesson."'

'Oh, God,' he sighed. 'God in heaven.'

'And so we'll be dancing,' Sarah told her trembling husband. 'Dancing and laughing, and whispering sweet nothings. "Charles makes a very pretty maid," Ryan will whisper in my ear. "He does, doesn't he?" I'll whisper back. "He's very obedient and helpful around the house, but it can be lonely sometimes without a real man in my life."'

'No,' Charles gasped, but Sarah just put her mouth closer to his ear and said, 'I'll smile over at you when I feel his hardness through our clothes, but I won't stop. In fact I'll hold him closer, let him know how much I like dancing with his strong arms around me, and that's when I'll do it, Charles, that's when I'll kiss him.'

Charles moaned and trembled, caught in the jaws of humiliation and shame, but Sarah just laughed at his distress, saying, 'Of course I'll kiss him, I won't he able to stop myself, and why should I stop? He's the better man, isn't he? He's beaten you in work, it's only right he beats you in love. And it will feel so good to kiss him like that – a long, slow, lingering kiss, our bodies moving to the music, knowing you're watching us – so lovely I'll have to take him upstairs to bed.'

'Noooo,' Charles wailed like a child, crushed yet hugely aroused by the thought of Sarah doing such a thing, and by the thought of everyone witnessing his humiliation.

'I'm sorry, but that's what I'll do. I'm a Mistress after all, I can do what I like.'

Once more he groaned as if from a pit of shame.

'Poor Charles,' Sarah said. 'It will hurt so much, and you'll cry so hard, but you'll understand, I know you will. He's a real man not a slave, not a panty wearing housemaid. Of course I want to take him to bed, of course I want him to fuck me. It can't be stopped, it's the way of the world. Tell me you understand.'

'Oh, God,' he gasped, utterly lost in her story.

'Tell me,' she insisted.

'I understand,' he said.

'I'm glad,' she said, her own arousal growing sharp and urgent, 'but you don't just understand, do you? It's more than that because you want him to fuck me. You want your Mistress to be fucked by a real man. You want her to have the pleasure you can't give her. Say it, Charles, say you want him to fuck me.'

'I w-want …' he stammered.

'All of it,' she commanded. 'Say it.'

'I want him to fuck you.'

'Say his name.'

'I c-can't.'

'Say it.'

'Ryan … Ryan Moore.'

'You want Ryan to fuck me?'

'Yes.'

'Like this?' she said, moving on top of him, and taking him inside her with a single, fluid motion of her hips.

Charles cried out in delight, and Sarah, deeply aroused, tugged his hair, and hissed in his ear, 'This is how Ryan will fuck me while you're downstairs in your little uniform … This is how we'll fuck at my party … This is how we'll fuck …'

Trapped beneath her, Charles pushed upwards with a desperate hunger, but Sarah matched him thrust for thrust, exulting in her power, part of her believing she really was fucking Ryan Moore and not her helpless slave.

'It will feel so good,' she gasped, as lost as Charles in the power of her story. 'To fuck him at last … The better man … The better lover … And he will be better than you, won't he?'

'Yes,' Charles gasped.

'Much better?'

'Yes.'

'Oh, God,' she gasped, filled with an animal hunger for the stronger male. 'He'll tear my dress, push me down on the bed ... He'll fuck me, oh God, he'll fuck me ... I'll come so hard and so loud everyone will hear ... Everyone at the party ... Oh God, I'll come so hard ...'

Lost to bliss, their cries merging in ecstasy, they plunged over the cliff together and lay barely conscious on the rocks below. They came round slowly as if waking from a dream, and held each other while their breathing slowed.

'Go to sleep, Charles,' Sarah murmured softly. 'I told you I'd be cruel, and I have been, but it was a lovely kind of cruel, and we'll do it again, I promise ... Again and again ... Go to sleep,' she whispered, but he was already asleep, and Sarah soon followed him, her entire being suffused with a euphoric sense of peace and joy.

NOW THAT Sarah had introduced Ryan Moore into her stories, Charles wanted more and more. Every story had to have Ryan in it, and every mention of his name cut Charles like a knife, but he craved the brutal sharpness of this new pain. Nothing could match the pleasure he derived from imagining being outdone by his rival in front of his wife and Mistress, and he lived for her tales of cruelty and betrayal.

Thrilled by her new weapon, Sarah began to weave tales of Ryan into her real life. Whenever she was going out she'd have Charles help her dress, and say, 'I want to look my best tonight, I'm meeting someone special,' or 'I'll wear my prettiest panties and stockings tonight, thank-you, Charles. I have a feeling he'll like me in stockings.'

Charles knew Sarah wasn't really seeing Ryan Moore, and yet he believed her tales as if they were true, and he'd wait in a frenzy of submissive passion for her to get home, and Sarah learned to put his passion to good use.

After a perfectly harmless and friendly night out with Louise and Rebecca, Sarah became a sultry temptress as soon as she got home.

'I'm exhausted,' she said, sitting in an armchair and crossing her lovely legs with a whisper of nylon. 'I was right, he did like me in stockings. My God, how he liked me, he's worn me out.'

'C-can I get you anything?' Charles said, trembling with jealous arousal, and unable to meet her mocking gaze.

'No, but you can do something for me,' she said, uncrossing her legs, astonished yet thrilled by what she was about to ask of him. 'He's left me sore. It's the nicest kind of sore, but it's painful all the same. I wonder if you might kiss me better,' she said, opening her legs so that her dress rode up her thighs. 'I'd like you to do that for me, Charles - heal and cleanse me, kiss away my pain. It would be such a lovely way to show your devotion.'

Appalled by the thought of kissing her so intimately after she'd been with her lover, and yet deeply, insanely aroused, Charles sank to his knees before his Mistress.

'You'll do this for me?' she asked, moved by his surrender.

'Yes,' he said softly, another tremor passing through him.

'After I've been with him?'

'Yes,' he said.

'If you do this, you'll do anything,' she said, a warning in her voice.

'Yes,' he said, longing to kiss her.

'Then kiss me,' she said as he pushed his head under her dress. 'But gently, so gently,' she told him, wondering what it would be like if she'd really been with Ryan Moore. 'That feels so good,' she sighed as he kissed her through the thin silk of her panties. 'It's lovely for a woman to have a lover and a slave, the loveliest feeling in the world.'

Thrilled by his kisses, she moved her panties to one side to let him have her nakedness. 'I'm so pleased with you, Charles,' she gasped as her pleasure mounted. 'And Ryan will be pleased too, I know he will … When I tell him … When I tell him you're such a good and obedient slave.'

MUCH AS her new game thrilled her, Sarah felt unnerved by the extremity of her dominance over Charles, and by the intrusion of Ryan Moore into their fantasy lives. The next evening on her way home from work, fearful that sex was taking control of her life as much as it was her husband's, she made up her mind to ease up on Charles, perhaps even take a break from being his Mistress. Taunting him about Ryan was too deep and cruel a humiliation, much as they both loved it, and she planned to let Charles fuck her that night, and give him back some dignity and manly pride – but fate had different plans. When she came into the kitchen she saw the large parcel on the breakfast bar. For a moment she wondered if Charles had disobeyed her, and bought her clothes or underwear, but then she remembered – it was the toys she'd instructed him to buy.

'Is this what I think it is?' she said, lifting the parcel and finding it pleasingly heavy. 'I think it might be,' she added, suddenly very excited, and forgetting in an instant her plan to ease up on her husband. 'When did it arrive?'

'Th-this morning,' he stammered.

'And you've waited all day without opening it?'

'I thought you'd want to do that.'

'That's very thoughtful of you, Charles. Shall I open it now?'

'If you like.'

'Then I will,' she said, taking scissors from the drawer and cutting open the well-wrapped parcel. 'Look at these,' she said in excitement as she pulled out the adjustable leather cuffs. 'They're so well made and the leather's so soft, I bet you can't wait to try them. And here's the chain,' she said pulling out different lengths of slim but strong-looking silver chain that gleamed like treasure. 'Think of all the different ways we can use them, and what's this?' she said, taking out a little pouch, and pulling it open to peer inside.

'Oh, my,' she said, 'I'd forgotten about this.'

'Wh-what is it?' he asked, a tremor in his voice.

'Can't you guess?'

'No,' he lied, his brain swimming.

'Oh, I'm sure you could if you tried,' she said, taking out the contents of the pouch and holding it up for her slave to see. 'It's what you chose, remember? A black rubber bit, like something you'd use on a horse to make it behave.'

Charles stared at the object in fascinated horror, and Sarah too felt shocked by the look and feel of the gag. Fantasy was one thing, but this was something else altogether. The object felt very real in her hand, heavy and powerful and more than a little sinister. This was an instrument of restraint with only one purpose – to allow one human being to deny speech to another, to take away a person's most fundamental right. This may be a toy, Sarah thought, but it had a very real power to punish and enslave.

'It fastens at the back of the head,' said Sarah. 'It has its own little buckle but look, it comes with a tiny padlock so I can lock it on you if I want.'

Suddenly fearful of the gag, she dropped it beside the chain and cuffs as if was a poisonous snake before taking another larger packet from the parcel.

'I think I know what this is,' she said, tearing open the packet. 'And it is,' she announced happily, holding up a neck collar and leash in the same soft, supple leather as the cuffs. 'Your collar and leash, Charles, isn't that lovely? You can be my puppy, and I'll be your owner.'

She saw the fear in his eyes, and she felt her own apprehension fade. He could be frightened for both of them, but she, his Mistress, would be fearless.

'They are frightening, I quite agree, when you see them lying there, and they're not just something on a screen,' she said. 'They're more like instruments of torture than toys, but I think we should try them straightaway. If we don't we'll put them away in a drawer and never find the courage to take them out again. Strip to your panties, Charles, and then I'll try them on you. Hurry up, now, I've made up my mind.'

Unable to resist her, and possessed by a dark excitement, Charles took off his shoes and clothes until he was standing in just the pretty lilac knickers she'd given him to wear that morning.

'Hands behind your back,' she said. 'For now, at least, until we discover what works best.'

Obediently he placed his hands behind his back and stood still while she clipped two of the cuffs together to form handcuffs before fastening them around his wrists.

'There,' she said, struck by a lightning flash of arousal so strong she clenched her thighs together to catch the wave of pleasure. 'Try and free your hands.'

He made a half-hearted attempt to get free, and then stood still, his head bowed in defeat.

'Try harder,' she admonished him. 'I want to know you really can't get free.'

He tugged harder against his restraints, and knew instantly he could never free himself no matter how hard he tried. The reality of his bondage struck him like a blow, leaving him dazed and light-headed.

'You really can't get free, can you?' she said, smiling to see him come erect in her panties. 'I like that, and I see you like it too,' she added, putting her hand on his erection, and rubbing it through the silky material of her knickers.

'This looks almost evil,' she said, taking up the hard rubber bit. 'We'd better try it now before I lose my nerve, don't you think?'

Charles just stared like a fool. Aroused and terrified in equal measure, he longed for her to gag him even as he prayed she'd never do such a thing.

'But I'll wash it first,' she said, going to the sink. 'There's no knowing where it's been. For all we know you may not be its first victim. Perhaps they try them first before sending them out.'

Laughing at the idea, Sarah washed the bit thoroughly in liquid detergent before rinsing it carefully, and turning back to Charles.

'Look at you, Charles,' she said. 'You're shaking like a leaf. Are you really so frightened?'

Unable to speak, he nodded his head.

'But you still want this, don't you?' she said, noting that, despite his shaking, his cock had grown very hard.

He stared at her, an animal in headlights.

'Say you want it even if it's just for my sake.'

His shaking grew worse, and he neither nodded nor shook his head.

'Say it, Charles,' she said, 'then I'll know I haven't forced you.'

He planned to say, 'No, I don't want it. Throw it away, I don't want to see the hellish thing ever again,' but instead he said, 'I want it.'

'That's wonderful,' she said, holding the bit to his mouth. 'Open wide.'

'Please, Sarah,' he said, changing his mind, 'I'm not sure we should …'

But Sarah just pushed the bit into his mouth, saying, 'Don't make a fuss,' and fastened the buckle behind his head before he could say any more.

'There,' she said, very aroused. 'We don't need the padlock with your hands tied like that. How does it feel?'

He made a foolish, choking sound.

'Of course,' she said, laughing at her stupidity. 'You can't speak, can you? And it looks very uncomfortable. I'm glad it's you and not me who's wearing it. Is it uncomfortable, Charles? You can nod or shake your head.'

He nodded his head emphatically, a panicked look in his eyes.

'Never mind,' she said, glorying in her new power, 'I'm sure you'll get used to it, but I want to hear you try to speak again. Say something for me. Thank-you, Mistress, try that.'

He tried to speak, the words coming out as "akoo ithreth."

'Oh, dear,' she laughed, 'you really can't speak, can you? I love you, Sarah, try that.'

His tongue impeded by the hard rubber bit, he could only manage, 'uvoo arra.'

'That's sweet,' she said. 'You sound just like a baby, now let's try your collar while we're at it.'

Deeply aroused to wield such power over him, Sarah fitted the collar around his neck, and fastened its buckle.

'Not too tight,' she said, checking she could get two fingers between the collar and his neck. 'I don't want to choke you. Oh, I like the look of that,' she said, stepping back to admire him in his bonds. 'You look like a slave in ancient Rome.'

Thrilled by his bound appearance, Sarah longed to reach under her skirt and touch herself, but she resisted the temptation. She wanted to appear cold, even a little bored with her slave. That was sexy too, to feign coolness when she was burning with excitement.

'You make a very handsome slave,' she told him. 'All the Roman ladies would be bidding against each other to take you home.'

He made another choking sound, and stared at her with a pleading look in his eyes.

'Don't worry,' she said, deliberately misinterpreting his look. 'I haven't forgotten your leash.'

She attached the leash to the ring on his collar with a satisfying click.

'Mmmmmth,' he protested, the foolish sound only arousing her, and making her tug his leash harder as she led him from the room.

Like a child with a new pet, Sarah had great fun leading Charles all round the house, going into every room before going upstairs to their bedroom. 'You don't really need a leash, do you?' she laughed, taking hold of the erection that bobbed in front of him. 'You come with your own leash. All men do. Maybe that's what these have been for all along,' she said, tugging him by his cock, 'leashes for women to lead men by.'

Still laughing, Sarah tethered him to the bedrail, seeing herself for a moment as a cowgirl tying her steed outside the saloon. 'There,' she said. 'I've tied you so you can't move. I'm going to leave you now. I want you to think about how things are now, about how I can do what I like with you. I can leave you here all evening if I want.'

He made another lowing sound, and took a step towards her but the leash held him, tugging his head back. Anger flared in his eyes, and he worked his arms in an effort to get free, but his bonds held firm.

'Don't pretend you don't like it,' she said, fondling his erection, deeply aroused that he could do nothing to stop her. 'You can't hide, Charles, I can see how much you like it. I want you to think of me downstairs getting on with my life. I'll have a meal, drink some wine. I may even go out, or invite someone round. I can do what I like, but all you can do is wait for your

Mistress. Bye-bye,' she said, tapping his erection so that it swayed from side to side. 'Enjoy yourself, I know I will.'

Charles stared after her helplessly as she walked towards the door, her lovely figure deeply alluring in her tight skirt and sheer hose. He couldn't believe she was leaving him like this, and his anger at her grew even stronger and yet, for all his rage and disbelief, his arousal knew no bounds, and he felt the deepest gratitude for her cruelty. If he'd been able to speak he could only have said, 'I love you, Mistress. I love you for all time.'

It gave Sarah the greatest pleasure to know Charles was her prisoner. As she ate the meal Charles had prepared for her, her stomach fluttered with excitement at the thought of her bound and gagged husband. She couldn't put her finger on what it was that excited her so much – perhaps it was knowing she'd rendered his life pointless while she was free to do as she liked. It even aroused her to think of how bored he must feel to be so trapped and helpless, and unable to speak or move, or think of anything except his cruel Mistress. Everything she did carried an extra thrill – whether it was eating or drinking, or calling her friends or watching TV or listening to music, or even going to the bathroom – because she knew Charles could no longer enjoy any of these simple freedoms. She'd taken them from him, and claimed them entirely as her own. He was her pet, her puppet, and she could do with him as she liked.

But her excitement wouldn't let her settle, and her thoughts turned more and more to the costume hidden in her wardrobe. 'It's too much,' she told herself, 'let him get used to being tied first,' but she couldn't let go of the idea, and soon she was climbing the stairs to her bedroom, her arousal growing more urgent with every step.

'Don't get your hopes up,' she told her wide-eyed slave when she came into the room. 'I'm not here to let you go. There's something else I'm going to try, but I'll have to get you ready first.'

Going to her dressing-table, she rummaged through the drawer that held her stockings and hose. 'I've found them,' she said, holding up a pair of black seamed tights. 'These will do nicely.'

Tossing her lovely, dark hair, she went over to her slave, and said, 'I'm going to put these on you, Charles. It might be easier if you sit on the bed.'

He made a garbled protest, but Sarah said, 'Don't try to speak. You only sound stupid. Now sit, unless you want me to make you.'

He stared at her furiously, and she was about to push him down on the bed when he sat of his own accord.

'That's more like it,' she said coldly. 'The next time I tell you to do something I expect you to do it straightaway.'

She rolled up the tights and carefully fitted them onto Charles' legs. When she'd got them as far as his thighs she instructed him to stand. This time he obeyed without hesitation, and she pulled the tights over his dainty little panties.

'Lovely,' she said, going behind him to adjust the seams of his hose so they ran neatly up the middle of his legs. 'You have nice legs, Charles. Any girl would be happy to have them.'

He stared at his wife in fear and incomprehension, the soft hose shamingly feminine and cool against his skin, but his silent distress only added to her pleasure. 'Now for your shoes,' she said, going to her shoe-store.

Charles watched in horror as she searched through her shoes, holding one pair against another to see which was biggest. 'I'm a size 5 and you're an 8 so this won't be easy,' she said. 'These might fit,' she said, holding up a pair of black court shoes with two-inch heels. 'They've always been big on me, and I've put a sole in them to make them fit. But if I take them out,' she added, taking out the soles and turning back to her slave, 'then they might just do.'

Kneeling, she held the shoes for Charles, and guided his feet into them. 'Push down,' she instructed him. It was a tight squeeze, but she managed with some difficulty to fit his feet into the shoes.

'Well done, Charles,' she praised him. 'I'm sure they're very uncomfortable, but a slave should suffer for his Mistress, don't you think? And knowing you, you'll enjoy the pain.'

A bizarre, pitiful figure, he stood precariously in his heels and seamed hose, as ungainly as an ostrich.

'We're not finished yet,' she told him. 'But I want the next bit to be a surprise, it will be much more fun that way. So close your eyes, Charles, and keep them closed until I tell you to open them.'

To her delight, he instantly obeyed, and Sarah experienced another spasm of raw female power. Overwhelmed, she clutched onto the bedrail as the wave of pleasure swept through her. Barely recovered, and every nerve-end still alive with delight, she went to the wardrobe and took the parcel from its hiding-place.

'No peeking now,' she told Charles as she placed the parcel on the bed and began to unwrap it, her hands trembling with excitement. 'I mean it, Charles, I'll be very angry if you look before I tell you.'

Deeply curious, Charles nevertheless kept his eyes tight shut. He couldn't speak, he couldn't move his arms, and now he couldn't see. How could this have happened to him? It wasn't possible, people just didn't behave like this, and yet he welcomed his ridiculous bondage. In some sick and deranged way, he'd never felt happier, or more in love.

'Lift your leg,' he heard Sarah command him, and he did as he was told, tottering on one high-heeled shoe. 'Careful, now,' she said, holding him. 'We don't want you falling.' He felt her put something over his foot, and then she said, 'Now the other foot.' He lifted his other foot and she put something over it, before pulling it up his legs right to his waist. It felt like another pair of knickers, a larger pair, but he couldn't be sure.

'One last thing, and then we're done,' she said, leaning in close and fixing something to his head. He smelled her perfume and felt her soft hair touch against his cheek as she went about her work, and he longed to open his eyes, but he kept them obediently closed. He felt a band grip him across the middle of his head, and he was certain she'd put him in cat's ears again. That wouldn't be so bad, he thought, he was used to that.

He heard her untie him from the bedrail, and felt a gentle tug on his leash. 'I'm going to move you now,' she said, 'but I want you to keep your eyes shut, and walk very carefully. You're not used to walking in heels, and we'll be going downstairs, so do everything I tell you. Is that clear?'

He nodded his head as she led him from the bedroom and out into the upstairs hall.

It felt strange and uncomfortable to be walking in painfully tight high-heeled shoes, and yet Sarah had been right – he did take pleasure in the pain, and he felt his cock stir and harden as he blindly followed his Mistress.

She gripped him firmly round his waist as she guided him step by step down the stairs, reminding him several times to keep his eyes closed. When they reached the bottom, she led him, not left towards the kitchen, but right towards the front-door, and he shivered in sudden fear. She couldn't be taking him outside, could she? Not onto the street where everyone could see him wearing high heels and panties and God knows what else she'd dressed him in?

He moaned in distress, and refused to move, shaking his head from side to side.

'It's alright,' she said, guessing the reason for his panic. 'I'm not taking you outside if that's what you're frightened of. One day perhaps, but not today.'

Hardly re-assured, he let her pull him forwards a few more steps, and then she stopped him, and he felt her tether his leash to something he couldn't see.

Sarah stepped back from her prisoner, and admired her work. She'd tethered him to one of the bannister rails, making sure he was facing the full-length hall mirror. That was an important part of her plan. She wanted him to see himself as soon as he opened his eyes. She wanted him to see what she had reduced him to. She wanted him to be shocked, and frightened and deeply shamed. She wanted him to feel the full extent of her power over him, and she wanted to experience the full thrill of that power.

'You can open your eyes now,' she told him, welcoming the heavenly wetness between her legs, and watching eagerly as he opened his eyes and regarded his reflection in the full-length mirror.

What Charles saw made him moan in shock and anger, and stagger forwards on his heels so that his collar choked him. To his horror, he saw that he was wearing a cheap and tawdry bunny-girl costume with pink full-cut panties and huge pink fur-lined rabbit's ears sticking up from his head. He tried to say something like 'What in God's name have you done?' but his gag only let him make a foolish babbling sound. He turned his shocked and furious gaze on Sarah but she just stroked his shoulder, and leaned in close, saying, 'Look what I've done to you, Charles. I've made you into my sweet, little bunny-girl. I'll call you Hopsy or Bugs, Brer or Bunny-Honey, and I'll dress you like this whenever I want, and I'll leave you tied up in the hall.

That way, if any guests come to the door, you'll be the first thing they see when they come into the house.'

She smiled to see the new terror come into his eyes.

'What a lovely surprise you'll give them,' she continued. 'Maybe I'll ring some people right now, invite them round. Perhaps I'll call Ryan, I'm sure he'd love to see you like this. Think how you'll feel when the doorbell rings. You'll jump out of your skin, but I won't care. In fact it will make me laugh as I walk past you to answer the door. "This is Hopsy," I'll say to Ryan after I've kissed him. "Doesn't he have the cutest ears, and the prettiest little cotton-tail?" Sarah turned Charles so he could see another detail of his costume reflected in the mirror – the little white fluffy ball sewn onto the back of his panties. 'I'll get you to wag your tail so Ryan can see how happy you are to see him. And then we'll leave you like this, and go upstairs to bed. The fun we'll have, thinking of our little bunny helpless in the hall.'

Charles made a snorting sound, and tugged hard on his leash which held fast and pulled his head back.

'Careful, now,' Sarah said. 'I don't want you hurting yourself, that's my job.'

Laughing at her silly joke, she kissed his scarlet cheek, and caressed him through the front of his panties, aroused to discover he was no longer erect.

'What's the matter, Hopsy? Have I frightened you? Have I been so cruel you're not enjoying yourself any more? But you like it when I'm cruel to you, and I'm sure you love being my bunny-girl. Come on, Hopsy,' she urged him, caressing him more firmly, 'show me how much you like it, show me how much you like your ears and your bunny-panties and your little fluffy tail. And your legs look so lovely in tights. Honestly, Charles, with legs like those you could be a show-girl. You could dance the can-can. So come on, show me how much you like it when I'm cruel to you. That's better,' she said in mocking approval when he came erect in his panties. 'Now you're a happy bunny. Now you're my bunny-honey.'

He moaned in helpless arousal, and pushed against her hand.

'Oh my, how you love your new costume,' she taunted him, 'but I'm going to leave you for a while so you can get used to your new look,' she told him, taking away her hand, and smiling at the outline of his erection beneath his panties. 'I want you to wait here and look at what I've done to you. I want you to know I own you body and soul, and can do whatever I like to you. I want you to know this is real and not a game.'

He stared at her pleadingly, a look of utter desperation in his big, brown eyes.

'Be seeing you,' she said, kissing him on the cheek and patting his fluffy little tail before turning and walking away down the hall. As she walked she swayed her hips in an exaggerated fashion. She knew it was a cheap and silly thing to do, and she'd never walked like this in her life, a sassy girl in a cartoon, but she couldn't help herself. It was fun, and she wanted him to experience the full force of her female power. She wanted him to desire her to the point of madness, and she wanted him to know she'd only satisfy his desire if and when it pleased her.

But her self-control vanished in an instant as soon as she went into the living-room. Then the full force of her arousal swept through her, and she pulled up her skirt and tugged down her panties and hose and threw herself onto the couch where she lay curled up with her hand between her legs. Pressing her face into a cushion to stifle her cries, she achieved an orgasm so sudden and explosive it left her dazed. As she drifted into sleep she wondered what it was about treating her husband so cruelly that excited her. She knew it was silly and childish of her to dress Charles in such a demeaning way, and yet she couldn't deny the pleasure it gave her. Had she always resented his power and privilege? Was she taking revenge on him for having everything in life she'd lacked in her childhood? She couldn't believe she was so vindictive, or that the reason for her behaviour was so obvious, but she could think of no other explanation other than that she truly had become a sadistic woman. 'Oh, well,' she told herself as her eyes grew heavy, 'you'll just have to live with it, and so will Charles.'

When she woke she sat up with a start and looked at her watch. She'd been asleep for over half an hour. As her thoughts slowly cleared, she felt certain she was dreaming, and was still asleep on the couch. She couldn't have done that to Charles, could she? She couldn't have dressed him so foolishly and left him tied up in the hall. She stood and pulled up her underwear and tugged her skirt into place and then, gripped by curiosity, she tiptoed to the door and peered into the hall.

What she saw amazed her. It wasn't possible, but there was Charles bound and gagged and tied to the bannister wearing a pink bunny-girl's costume with a little fluffy tail and huge ears, his feet in a pair of her high-heeled shoes, and his legs encased in seamed hose. Charles Hunter, her wealthy husband and, until recently a powerful and successful executive in charge of Joseph & Hill Investment, had been reduced to a figure of fun, an object of scorn and ridicule.

Unaware of her presence, Charles was staring at his ridiculous reflection with a horrified expression on his face. What's more, one of his bunny ears had bent over in the middle, giving him a very forlorn and comical appearance.

Sarah's heart went out to him, not as a real person suffering real pain and degradation, but as a creature she had willed into existence.

Her creature.

'Poor Hopsy,' she said coming towards him, and smiling to see him start in fear. 'One of your ears has gone all floppy. Maybe I should call you Flopsy instead of Hopsy.'

Reaching him, she stroked his shoulder to calm him, and caressed the strap of the gag where it dug into his cheek.

'I'm sorry to leave you for so long,' she said, aroused once more by the fear and anger in his eyes, 'but I've been having a snooze. I know, I know, I'm a very cruel Mistress to fall asleep when you're in such a state, but there you go, that's the kind of woman I've become.'

She straightened his ear, and laughed when it bent over again. Then she hugged him, running her hands over his bound wrists, and breathing in the new leather smell of his collar, a scent she found intoxicating. A shiver ran through him, and she shivered too, tuning into his fearful excitement.

'I like the smell of your collar,' she said. 'And it's lovely to know I can do this to you. I've gone mad, I know I have. Why else would I enjoy treating you this way? Why else would I even think of doing such a thing?'

Crooking a leg around one of his, she slid her leg up and down, enjoying the sweet friction of nylon against nylon. 'How pretty your leg feels,' she said. 'So soft and smooth in your tights. Does mine feel the same? I'm sure it does.'

He gave another shiver, and she stroked his cheek fondly, saying, 'Poor Charles, your wife has turned into a very cruel woman, but I'm going to untie you now. But before I do, let's make sure you're ready to be untied.'

Looking into his eyes, she began to caress him through his panties and hose, saying, 'Come on, I want you nice and hard. Show me how much you love and adore me. Show me you're not going to be angry.'

He tottered on his heels, and a pained look came into his eyes, and yet she felt him come obediently erect.

'Harder, Hopsy,' she said in a mocking tone that made him grow even harder. 'As hard as you can.'

He moaned into his gag, and pushed against her hand.

'That's the way,' she said, thrilled by his servile arousal. 'Now I know you forgive me for being cruel to you. And you do forgive me, don't you, Charles?'

Anger blazed in his eyes, and yet he nodded his head.

'Then here are your instructions. When I untie your hands you'll put your arms around me in a gentle and loving hug. And when I take off your gag I want to hear no angry words, no complaints or recriminations. On the contrary, there are only four words you are permitted to say to me, and those are, "I love you, Mistress." Have I made myself clear?'

Once more he nodded his head, but his eyes had misted with tears, and she felt fearful when she untied his leash and unbuckled his cuffs. Would he attack her? Would he strike her for making him look so foolish, and treating him so cruelly? But she needn't have worried. As soon as he was free, he embraced her tenderly, almost falling against her as he pressed his face into her fragrant hair.

Sarah smiled to feel his erection push against her. 'That's my lovely slave,' she said, unfastening the cruel bit, and taking it from his mouth. 'Now then, Charles, is there something you wish to say to me?'

'I love you, Mistress,' he said, tears of love and gratitude falling from his eyes.

CHARLES KNEW he had to do something. Every day, when Sarah was at work, he planned ways to break her hold over him, and take back his place in the world as a free man. He recalled his old freedom and identity most powerfully when he took physical exercise. Using the machines in the gym reminded him of his male pride and vigour, and surging up and down the pool made him feel strong and decisive. As he swam, he saw himself standing up to Sarah, and refusing to live any longer as her slave and yet, after he dried himself in his cubicle at the swimming-baths, it was her panties he pulled up his legs, and their soft lace imprisoned him as tightly as any cuff or collar. And, when he got home, all it took was the sight of her coats hanging in the cloakroom, or her clothes and underwear in the laundry-room, or her photograph on the table in the living-room, for his slavery to begin anew. And then, as the time for her to return from work grew nearer, his submissive arousal grew so strong that he'd rush to answer the door to her, and throw himself at her feet.

He no longer minded having to keep silent until she told him he could speak. In fact it thrilled him to serve in enforced silence, and he even looked forward to the times she gagged him with the bit. For all the discomfort it caused him, it made him feel subdued and owned in a way that eased his anxiety, and helped him accept his servitude as well as the burden of existence. And when she dressed him in his ridiculous bunny ears and panties, and bound him in his cuffs and collar, and tethered him in the hall, or in their bedroom or the cupboard containing the vacuum and cleaning equipment, or in the laundry-room with nothing to do except watch her laundry go round and round in the washing-machine, or in the bathroom where she used the toilet in front of him without paying him the slightest heed as if he was no more than a statue, Charles felt as if he'd found his true place in life.

And he looked forward to Mistress-Time every Sunday night with an almost religious fervour. In the most recent session, Sarah had smiled down at his naked form, and praised him generously.

'I really couldn't be happier,' she'd told him. 'You do everything I tell you without complaint even if it causes you the greatest shame and discomfort. I'm amazed this has happened to us, Charles, and I'm sure you are too, but happen it has, and we must make the most of it, and not fight against our true natures. I'm particularly pleased by how you've accepted my need to take a lover.'

Sarah didn't say this just to be cruel. By mentioning his imaginary cuckolding in the context of Mistress-Time she was moving it from being an ingredient in her night-time stories, and making it a very real possibility in their day-to-day lives as Mistress and slave. She was preparing the ground for her to really take a lover. It was a prospect that frightened her – she didn't want to risk ruining her marriage – and yet taking a lover now felt like the inevitable next step in her life as a dominant woman, and it carried an erotic force she found irresistible. She didn't have anyone in mind, for all she terrorised Charles with tales of Ryan Moore, but she wanted Charles to accept her right to go with other men. That way, if she found someone, she could proceed quickly and with a clear conscience. She wouldn't have to tell any stupid lies.

'Isn't it strange how things work out?' she said to her kneeling slave. 'What once seemed impossible now feels inevitable, almost normal. Of course I can go with other men if I want. I'm a Mistress, I can do what I like. But not you, Charles. As a slave you must remain utterly faithful to me. It's terribly unfair, I know, but I'm afraid that's the burden you have to bear, and I'm sure you'll find solace in thinking of my pleasure. And it will give me pleasure to go with other men, and with Ryan in particular, I want you to know that. In fact, thinking of you waiting at home for me adds immeasurably to my pleasure, and Ryan will find it positively inspiring, I'm sure. It's lovely to have found such a special and unexpected freedom in my life, and I'm very grateful to you for helping me find it.'

She was doing it again – talking about Ryan Moore as her lover, and once more she saw the effect it had on Charles, the way it made him wince in distress even as his cock grew harder. And it aroused her too, made her shift in her chair, and think of Ryan's handsome face and strong, steady eyes.

She told herself she should stop using Ryan in this way, and yet imagining him as her lover aroused her and Charles like nothing else. Almost every night she taunted Charles with tales of her make-believe dates with Ryan, and of the pleasure she took in their love-making. Charles knew these were only stories, but they carried a formidable power, and brought him a masochistic delight he feared he couldn't live without. And he saw how much the stories aroused Sarah, and that only heightened his arousal. He could tell she wanted the stories to come true and, to his shame, he had grown to want the same thing.

He was well aware that Sarah barely knew Ryan, and yet he began to dread the possibility of them becoming lovers. It was a sweet and erotic dread, but it haunted his imagination with relentless power, and he wanted rid of it before it spread through every part of him like a disease.

And so, alarmed by the depth of his submission to Sarah, Charles made a further bid for freedom. His daily job-search found an advert for a Chief Executive position with a leading finance company, and Charles decided to apply for it, but Sarah's response to his intention left him stunned.

'No,' she said bluntly, not even looking up from the book she was reading.

'What do you mean?' he asked, arousal already sweetening his shock.

'No, you can't apply, what did you think I meant?'

'But I have to apply, it's got my name all over it.'

'That's as maybe, but I don't want you to apply.'

'That's crazy, I stand every chance of getting it.'

'I don't care.'

'I need to get back to work, Sarah, you know I do.'

'I know nothing of the kind, Charles,' she said, putting down her book, and gazing at him sternly.

'I can't go on living like this, it's not possible.'

'That's no longer your decision, Charles. I'm sure you know that in your heart of hearts.'

'Please, Sarah,' he said, angry at himself for sounding so weak. 'Just let me send in my CV.'

'No, Charles, that won't be happening,' she told him firmly. 'And it won't be happening because I won't let it happen.'

'But why?' he asked, wishing his voice had held steady.

'Because I don't give you my permission.'

'Then give me your permission.'

'No, Charles, I won't.'

'Why not, for God's sake?'

'Because I'm happy with the way things are,' she said with a brazen confidence that chilled him. 'I enjoy being the lady of the house and having a slave run after me hand and foot, and I'm not going to give that up. And you're not a free man any more. You really are my slave, you need to accept that. I truly am the head of this household, and my word is law. You won't be applying for the job, Charles, so you can put the idea out of your head.'

'Sarah ...' he started to object.

'I forbid it, and that's my final word.'

'This is insane.'

'I'm warning you, Charles,' she said in a very severe tone, 'I'll hear no more about it.'

'You can't do this,' he said.

'I've heard quite enough,' she said, her voice suddenly sharp with anger. 'Go and stand in the corner until you learn some manners. Go on, this minute, I won't tell you again.'

His head spinning, and amazed at how spineless he'd become, Charles went obediently to the corner where he stood with his face pressed against the wall. It was bad enough that she'd denied him the chance to apply for a job, but now she was punishing him as if he was a small child. It was entirely unjust of her, a needlessly cruel display of tyranny. 'Hands behind your back,' she instructed him. As he obeyed, Charles, to his despair, felt himself come erect. Not only did he lack the strength to stand up to her, but it gave him pleasure to surrender so meekly. The thought made him begin to shake. 'Look at you,' Sarah said, a very real contempt in her voice. 'You're shaking like a baby. It wouldn't surprise me if you were crying. Are you, Charles, are you crying?'

'N-no,' he answered, the word sounding like a sob.

'You are crying,' she said cruelly. 'I can hear it in your voice, but don't expect me to feel sorry for you. Your outburst has made me angry, and you'll stay there until I can think of a suitable punishment.'

She left him like that for nearly an hour before calling to him, 'Come over here, Charles, I need to take your measurements.'

Still shaking, and with his heart in his mouth, Charles left his punishment corner and went to his Mistress who took his measurements briskly with a white dress-tape. 'Just as I thought,' she said, 'somewhere between a 14 and a 16. Now, come and sit beside me, there's something I want to show you.'

He sat fearfully on the couch beside her and looked at the laptop screen balanced on her knees.

'As you can see,' she said, amused by his distraught expression, 'I'm looking at maid's uniforms. I've talked about getting you one for long enough, and your display of petulance has persuaded me you need a further reminder of your position in my house, although I have a feeling you may come to see it more as a reward than a punishment This one on the screen is my favourite. I think it might suit you very well. It's very smart and neat, don't you think?'

Charles stared at the image on the screen of a slim and smiling young woman wearing a black maid's dress with short white-trimmed sleeves and a little white apron. He tried to speak, and beg her not to buy him the uniform, but his mouth was dry and, greatly to his shame, he found the idea of being made to wear such a dress deeply and disturbingly erotic.

'What's the matter?' said Sarah. 'Has the cat got your tongue?'

'P-please ...' he stammered weakly.

'Please what?' she said impatiently. 'Please buy me the dress or please don't buy it?'

'Please d-don't,' he managed to say, fighting off his shameful arousal.

'Don't be silly,' she said, selecting a size 16. 'Of course I'm going to buy it. In fact, I'm going to buy you two dresses, one in black like the one on the screen, and another in blue. Then you'll have one to wear when the other's in the wash. And I've already selected a pair of wide-fitting black court shoes in a size 7. It's the biggest size they have, I'm afraid, but they'll be much more comfortable than any pair of mine. So cheer up, Charles, I'm sure you'll love dressing as my maid, and it'll be nothing compared to wearing your bunny costume. Well, then, what do you say?' she added with a knowing smile.

'Thank-you, Mistress,' he said, his gut churning with masochistic delight.

'You're very welcome,' she said. 'I'm sure you'll work even harder in your dresses, but you can buy them,' she added, handing him her lap-top. 'I know how much you like buying gifts for me, and besides, I like to think of you sealing your own fate. It makes everything so much more fun, don't you think?'

His hands shaking, and barely able to breathe, Charles entered his payment details, and sealed his fate.

WHEN HIS uniform dresses and shoes arrived only four days later, Sarah wasted no time in dressing Charles in his new uniform. Wearing a maid's dress shamed Charles unbearably, and yet a part of him wore the dress happily, almost proudly, thrilled by how meek and subservient it made him feel. Dressing as a maid in real life proved even more pleasurable than it had in Sarah's stories, particularly when Sarah taught him to curtsey neatly and precisely, and insisted he perform the servile act whenever he came into her presence. She also bought him a six-pack of cheap tights at the lingerie shop in the station, telling him, 'I'm not wasting my good nylons on the maid. You'll still wear my dirty panties every day, but you can wear your own tights.' She looked out a waist-slip with a lace hem that fitted neatly under his dress, and flashed prettily white with every step he took. Whenever Charles looked down and saw his apron and sheer nylons, and his pretty shoes and the little flashing hem of his slip, his insides turned over with shameful excitement, and he experienced the delicious drowning sensation he'd come to crave with the hunger of an addict.

He put on his uniform in the hour before Sarah's return from work, and he'd stare at his reflection in the hall mirror, fascinated by his effeminate appearance, blushing with shame as he practised his curtsey.

Whenever Sarah saw him in his uniform she couldn't help but giggle, to begin with at least. But she soon grew accustomed to seeing him in his maid's dress, and before long even the sight of him curtseying had come to seem almost normal.

'Honestly, Charles,' she said, 'you look so pretty in your uniform, and you take such neat, small steps these days, just like a girl, and you curtsey so sweetly, I really do think of you as my maid. I certainly no longer think of you as a man, and I can hardly remember what it was like when you were my husband.' Sarah was so thrilled with his transformation into her feminised housemaid that she insisted he wear his uniform every evening unless they had guests, which wasn't often, and after a few weeks she took things further by buying him two wigs to wear with his dresses – one dark-coloured in a neat bob cut, and the other a shoulder length wig in blond curls.

She thought he suited both, and couldn't decide which one she preferred, so she instructed him to wear the blond wig with his blue maid's dress, and his black wig with his black dress. In his blond wig and blue dress she amused herself by thinking of him as her Swedish au-pair, and in his black wig and uniform she thought of him as her French soubrette.

Charles had little hair on his body, and Sarah decided against shaving him, although she insisted he keep his face freshly shaved at all times, which meant he had to shave twice a day, once in the morning when he rose to make her breakfast, and again in the late afternoon before she got home from work. She also thought long and hard about putting him in make-up, but in the end decided against it, telling him, 'You'd pass as a woman if I did your make-up carefully, but I don't want you to pass as a woman. I want you to look like a man trapped in a dress. Don't ask me why, but it's much sexier that way.'

One afternoon, in the chemist's after work buying some new make-up, Sarah saw on the shelves a cheap body-spray she remembered wearing as a young teenager. Called 'Charlie,' the spray had a strong, over-sweet scent which she immediately knew would be perfect for her maid. And, of course, its brand-name was too perfect to resist.

'You'll wear this every day,' she informed him when she got home, spraying the scent on his neck and wrists. 'That way you'll smell as sweet as you look. Make sure to let me know when it runs out, and I'll buy you another.' She even took to calling him Charlie after the scent instead of Charles. She knew he'd always hated this diminutive version of his name, and yet, such was the way of sadomasochism, he soon thrilled to the sound of the name, and every evening when he put on his maid's dress and applied his scent before Sarah's return from work, he experienced a powerful surge of masochistic arousal that lingered with his scent as he scurried in the service of his Mistress.

'Admit it,' Sarah instructed her blushing maid, 'you love wearing your uniform with your pretty wigs and sweet-smelling scent.'

'I love it,' he confessed helplessly, fearing he might faint from the shame of it.

'Then what do you say?' she said with her creamiest smile.

'Th-thank-you, Mistress,' he said from the depths of his being.

'This is wonderful,' said Sarah. 'I feel as if I own you, and can do whatever I like with you. I've said it before, and I'll say it again. It's like magic, truly it is.'

After wearing his uniform-dresses and wigs every night for almost two weeks, it came as a huge relief to Charles to be going out with Sarah to a party as her husband, and wearing his man's clothes for once. Sarah's boss Alan Rennie was holding a celebration at his house to mark the thirtieth anniversary of the company, and Charles was expected to attend as Sarah's partner. Only staff and their spouses, and valued clients would be attending, and so Charles expected a fairly relaxed affair, but Sarah reminded him of his subordinate position by insisting he wear her panties under his trousers, and by spraying him with his cheap scent, and by calling him Charlie in front of her friends and colleagues at the party. And Sarah looked wonderful in the ruby-red velvet dress she'd bought for the occasion – the colour showing off her shining dark hair to great advantage and its knee-length style making the most of her naturally good legs, and Charles couldn't help noticing how men kept casting sly glances in her direction. Women too, Charles observed, suspecting they were envious of her stylish good looks.

Sarah had always been pretty in a slightly plump and unexceptional way, but in the last year or so she seemed to have shed her puppy fat, if that was possible in a woman of 47, and become slimmer, almost coltish. Her face looked slimmer too, her features prouder and more sculpted. She hadn't dieted or taken exercise, she must have simply grown into her looks, Charles decided, but he wondered if it was her newfound confidence as his Mistress that had transformed her into such a beautiful and captivating woman. In a way Charles couldn't explain, she now filled the eye with a grace and symmetry she'd never possessed before and, wherever she went at the party, she became the centre of attention.

Charles wasn't drinking alcohol as he was Sarah's chauffeur for the evening, but he made do with mineral water and fruit juice. He didn't know many people there, but he was acquainted with enough of them to always have someone to talk to, and even though he was on the periphery, very much in Sarah's shadow, he began to relax and even enjoy himself a little. But then something happened that shattered his calm, and sent his brain reeling.

Ryan Moore walked into the room. He was on his own, tall and handsome in dark blue trousers and a blazingly white shirt, but it wasn't long before Alan Rennie and his wife Rachel went to welcome Ryan, talking and laughing with him, and treating him very much as a VIP. Charles immediately looked over to where Sarah was standing in a small group, and he saw that she too had spotted Ryan's arrival and was looking over at him. He saw her raise her head like a wolf catching a scent, and then toss her hair and subtly alter her body position so that she seemed to grow taller in a way that made her new dress fit tighter over her breasts and hang more alluringly against her legs, and then she turned her head and looked straight back at Charles, a strange and unreadable expression on her face.

Charles felt giddy, as if he'd plunged into a dream, or was living in one of Sarah's stories. The cheap scent Sarah had sprayed on him suddenly smelled overpoweringly strong – so strong that he felt certain everyone around him could also smell it – and he felt acutely aware of the woman's panties he was wearing under his trousers. He felt himself blush as the sickly sweet arousal coursed through his veins leaving him weak and confounded. What was going on? Why was Ryan Moore at the party? Had he and Sarah somehow conjured his appearance out of their imaginations, from their deepest and most depraved desires? As far as he knew Ryan had absolutely nothing to do with ACM Accountancy. Did Sarah know he would be coming? Is that why she'd paid so much for her new dress, and spent so long fixing her hair and doing her make-up? He suddenly feared that the tales of her dates with Ryan Moore hadn't been make-believe at all, and she really was having an affair with his arrogant and successful rival. Feeling an urgent need to talk to Sarah, he started to make his way towards her through the crowded room, but people spoke to him on the way, slowing his progress, and, whenever he got close to Sarah, she'd moved on to join another group of her colleagues, her head often thrown back in laughter and enjoyment. He felt increasingly helpless, as if he was moving through quicksand, or the Gods of ancient Greece had doomed him for all eternity to pursue his lovely wife without ever being able to reach her side.

But Charles was brave and determined, and he defied the Gods, and caught up with Sarah just as she was turning away from a circle of friends.

'Sarah,' he said, panic in his voice. 'We need to talk.'

'Whatever's the matter?' she said, leading him to a quiet corner of the room. 'You look terrible. Are you unwell?'

'Did you know he'd be here?' he asked, ignoring her question.

'Who?'

'Who do you think?'

'Oh, you mean Ryan, don't you?'

'Of course I do.'

'Well, what about him?' she said impatiently, smiling at someone over his shoulder in a way that made him feel small and insignificant.

'Did you know he'd been invited?'

'Yes, Alan told me last week he'd be coming.'

'Why didn't you tell me?'

'You wouldn't have come if I'd told you, and besides, I wanted to surprise you,' she said, a mischievous gleam in her eyes.

'But why's he here?'

'Ryan's thinking of hiring us as Brexit consultants to Joseph & Hill, and apparently that's largely due to my report. It would be a huge feather in my cap if they become a client, and Alan's asked me to be very nice to Ryan, not that that will be difficult – I'd forgotten how handsome he is.'

'I'd like to leave,' Charles said, feeling trapped and breathless.

'Don't be silly,' she said. 'We've only just got here.'

'Please, Sarah.'

'No, Charlie, we're not leaving. Now try to behave, and whatever you do, don't fall out with Ryan. If you put your mind to it, you may even enjoy yourself.'

And with that she was gone, leaving him in her wake as she joined another group of friends. Feeling abandoned and deeply anxious, Charles looked around only to see Ryan watching him from across the room with a faint smile on his face. Charles held his gaze, trying to look calm and strong, but he felt the heat rise within him, and he was the first to look away, hurrying out of the room in search of a bathroom.

Safely locked in the bathroom, Charles stood at the sink and splashed his face with cold water, but it did nothing to ease his anxiety which was somehow making him aroused – not in any ordinary way for his cock remained soft in his panties, but deep down in his gut where a dark and poisonous excitement had taken root. He tried to think about ordinary things but all he could see was Ryan's smile, and Sarah's lovely head lifting and turning to look over at Ryan. He saw again her dress tighten over her breasts as her eyes flashed with interest in his handsome rival. He felt a terrible dread of them meeting and talking and dancing, and yet he knew it was inevitable and, much worse, a part of him longed for them to find each other. Ryan looked so strong and assured, and Sarah's elegant beauty lit up the party. Who was he to come between them? They deserved each other while he deserved only to be mocked and ignored, and left to survive their passion in whatever way he could.

Urging himself to fight his sick excitement, he once more splashed water against his face, and made himself take deep, slow breaths in an attempt to drive away his ruinous thoughts, yet they persisted, and his cheap scent only smelled stronger, and he felt even more aware of the woman's panties he was wearing under his trousers. They were in a light pink shade with a pretty lace trim, and he remembered Sarah's mocking smile when she'd caught sight of them when he was putting on his trousers. 'Perfect,' she'd said with satisfaction, turning her head to do her make-up in her dressing-table mirror. 'You won't forget who you are wearing such pretty knickers. Not for one second will you forget that I'm your Mistress, and you're my slave.'

Aroused by the memory, Charles experienced a sudden terror that Sarah would tell Ryan he was wearing her knickers, and the terrible thought sparked an even darker terror – a deeply shameful vision of him dressed in his maid's uniform serving drinks to Sarah and Ryan while they sat kissing on the couch in his living-room at home. He saw Ryan run his hand under Sarah's dress, caressing her thighs and the tops of her stockings before reaching between her legs to make the delightful discovery that she was naked beneath her dress. 'I'm not wearing panties, darling,' she told Ryan in his vision, opening her legs wantonly to her lover. 'My maid's stolen them, I'm afraid. Charlie's always stealing my panties. He's wearing them under his uniform now, the little thief. Would you like to see them? If you want, I'll ask Charlie to lift up his dress, and show you his panties. I'm sure he'd love you to see. He looks so sweet in them you'd hardly know he was a man at all. Shall I ask him, darling?'

The terrible vision deepened Charles' arousal, and he felt himself stir and harden in his knickers just as someone tried the bathroom door, causing him to jump with fright. He quickly dried his face and hands, and left the bathroom, muttering his apologies to the woman who was waiting outside. Charles wasn't a religious man, yet he said a prayer as he crossed the hall towards the main party room. 'Please, God,' he prayed, 'let me get through tonight. Let me not give in to my terrible weakness. Let me rise above it, and keep hold of my pride and strength. Let me be a man.'

When he stepped into the room he was greeted by a blast of loud music. The dancing had begun, and four or five couples immediately took to the floor. To his relief, Sarah and Ryan were not among them, but when he looked over at Sarah he saw Ryan approach her and ask her to dance. To Charles' despair, Sarah smiled in acceptance and followed Ryan onto the floor. They moved well together, making an exceptionally good-looking couple, and Charles, crippled by jealousy, couldn't take his eyes off them.

As he watched them dance he experienced the same sick excitement he felt when listening to Sarah's stories of dancing with Ryan at her party, and a new fear took hold in him – the fear that they would kiss as they always did in Sarah's stories, and then go upstairs together to find a bed. He told himself Sarah would never do such a thing, not at a work party where she had her professional reputation to consider, but he couldn't shake off the fear, and the exquisite pain it caused him. He took a long drink of mineral water, wishing it had been alcohol, and when he looked back at the dance-floor Sarah was looking back at him, a knowing smile on her face. And then Ryan said something in her ear that made her laugh and lose herself in their dance again.

Charles was almost relieved when Alan Rennie appeared by his side, and spoke to him about Sarah.

'I don't know what tablets your wife's on,' he said, 'but I want some of them.'

Charles made himself laugh at the crass remark.

'She's a force of nature,' he replied.

'She's all that and more,' said Alan. 'I've never seen her look so well, and her recent work with the firm has been splendid. She used to be so quiet and timid, but she's come right out of her shell, and long may it last.'

'She's always worked hard,' said Charles, 'and now she's reaping the rewards.'

'We're all reaping the rewards,' said Alan, patting Charles on the shoulder as he moved on to speak to another of his guests. 'You're a lucky man, Charles, a very lucky man.'

But Charles didn't feel lucky as he stood watching his wife dancing with his greatest rival. He felt weak and queasy and, when they began their third dance in a row, he even thought of cutting in on them, but he lacked the courage. What if they refused? What if Sarah just laughed at him, and went back to dancing with Ryan?

But then, greatly to his relief, the song finished and Sarah and Ryan drifted slowly from the dance-floor, talking and laughing companionably as they went. Charles craned his head and stood on tiptoe, desperate for Sarah to notice him, and come over to join him, but she didn't so much as look in his direction, and she and Ryan joined up with another couple and stood talking with them. Charles told himself to go over and join them, but he couldn't bear the thought of meeting Ryan and, more than that, he didn't want to come between Sarah and Ryan. He wanted them to be together. He wanted them to become lovers. It was crazy, he knew, but that didn't make it any less true. Utterly lost and helpless, he looked round for something to distract him. Across the hall in another room he saw Rachel Rennie laying out food on a long table. She looked anxious and harassed, and he went to help her.

'Can I be of any help?' he asked Rachel.

'Oh yes, thank-you, Charles, you can,' she said gratefully. 'There are two large tureens in the kitchen. Would you be a dear and carry them through for me?'

Charles lifted them through and placed them on the table by a huge bowl of rice, and a tray of baked potatoes. The rest of the table was laid with salad and cold meats and cheeses as well as a mouth-watering array of breads and pickles. A smaller table was laden with puddings and desserts.

'Is there anything else I can do?' he asked Rachel.

'As a matter of fact, there is,' she said. 'If you don't mind.'

'I don't mind in the slightest,' he said.

'It's meant to be a buffet,' said Rachel, 'but I wonder if you'd serve the hot food for me?'

'Of course,' said Charles.

'You're an angel,' said Rachel. 'The rice goes with the curry, and the potatoes with the stew. Susan and I will see to the rest.' Susan was her teenage daughter who looked miserable, and bored out of her mind.

Feeling better for having something to do, Charles laid out his serving-spoons.

'I can't have you getting your clothes in a mess,' said Rachel, taking something from a drawer in a nearby cupboard. 'Sarah would never forgive me.'

Before he could stop her, Rachel was pulling a full-length apron over his head. It was a blue unisex apron but all the same it made him feel weak and foolish.

'It's alright,' Charles protested. 'I don't need to …'

'I insist,' Rachel said firmly, tying the apron at his waist. 'There, now, I won't have to worry.'

When Rachel turned away to instruct her daughter in her duties, Charles reached behind his waist to untie his apron, but his hands were trembling and he couldn't untie the knot. Cursing under his breath, he kept trying, but with no success, and then the guests began to filter through from the party-room looking for food, and he had no option but to commence serving them.

The guests as they filed past were friendly and polite, and no-one made any remark about his apron. Charles kept looking along the slow-moving line, dreading the arrival of Sarah and Ryan, but there was no sign of them, and he began to hope they'd decided not to eat, but then he saw them join the queue, standing a little too close to each other, and laughing and speaking intimately as if they were a couple.

As they drew closer he became queasy with anxiety, and he could barely look Ryan in the eye when he drew level with him.

'Glad to see you're keeping busy,' said Ryan.

'Curry or stew?' said Charles, not rising to the bait.

'Neither,' said Ryan. 'I'll stick to salad, but I'd like a baked potato, thank-you, Charlie.'

Ryan had never called him Charlie before, and his use of the name cut him like a knife.

'It's Charles,' he said, looking to assert himself.

'I do beg your pardon,' said Ryan, doing no such thing. 'But Sarah's been referring to you as Charlie, so I thought I should follow her lead.'

Swallowing back his anger, Charles served the potato onto Ryan's plate and glared accusingly at Sarah who just smiled at him as if nothing was out of the ordinary.

'The curry smells wonderful,' she said, 'I think I'll try that, but not too much rice.'

As Charles served the food onto her plate, Ryan said to Sarah, 'I'm very impressed, is he this helpful at home?'

'He's a godsend,' said Sarah, smiling at Charles. 'The perfect little housekeeper, you've no idea. He keeps everything very neat and tidy, and I never have to lift a finger around the house. He even does my ironing.'

Charles felt his temper rise, yet arousal twisted in his gut.

'I'm glad to hear it,' said Ryan, moving on so that Charles was alone for a moment with Sarah who leaned over and whispered in his ear.

'I'm very pleased with you, Charlie. Keep up the good work, and you may even earn a reward.'

And then she'd moved on to join Ryan, leaving Charles in a fever of anger and arousal.

After serving food to the guests, Charles helped Rachel and her daughter gather up the dirty plates and cutlery and stack them in the kitchen. When he took off his apron, Rachel kissed him gratefully on the cheek, and said, 'Sarah has you well-trained, I must say,' causing Charles to start in alarm, but he quickly understood she'd meant nothing by it. 'I couldn't have managed without you,' she added sincerely. 'You can come anytime.'

Strangely lifted by her praise, he went into the main party room and took up a position in a far corner of the room where he could observe the gathering without feeling too much part of it. Other men joined him from time to time singly and in pairs, and chatted with him about cars and politics and football. One of them was a Liverpool fan like Charles, and together they sang the praises of the current team, and of Klopp and Salah in particular, but most of the time Charles kept to himself, free to feed his masochistic hunger by watching Sarah and Ryan.

Sarah didn't dance only with Ryan, but she danced with him more than anyone else, and she didn't spend all her time in his company but, whenever she was apart from him, it wasn't long before she drifted to his side again, and they laughed a lot, and leant in close when they spoke, and gave every impression of being attracted to each other. Charles also watched the people around them, worrying that they'd notice how much time Sarah and Ryan were spending together, but no-one else seemed remotely interested in Sarah and Ryan.

To the other guests, Sarah was just a lovely, vivacious woman having a good time at a party, but Charles knew better. He knew she was aware of him watching her, and he could tell she enjoyed making him suffer. At one point he saw her put a hand on Ryan's chest and look up into his eyes, and he felt sure they were going to kiss, but she merely said something in his ear that made him laugh, and then stepped back again, but she immediately glanced over at Charles to make sure he'd been watching, and Ryan looked over at him too, and Charles feared that he'd understood Sarah's power over him, and the pleasure she found in tormenting him.

Another time, when they were dancing, Sarah seemed to fall against Ryan, and he held her protectively for long moments before letting go of her. Soon after they went back to their drinks where they stood awkwardly without speaking, as if something embarrassing had taken place, but it wasn't long before other guests joined them and all seemed well again.

It was well after twelve when Sarah finally came to speak to Charles.

'Are you having a good time?' she asked him insolently, not drunk but a little the worse for wear. Charles had noticed she'd never been without a glass of wine in her hand.

'It's late,' said Charles. 'Can't we go home?'

'Of course not,' said Sarah. 'I'm having much too lovely a time, and I've promised Ryan one last dance.'

'Not again,' he said. 'People will notice.'

'It's only you who notices.'

'Please, Sarah, I'm bored.'

'Don't lie,' she said with a knowing look. 'You're not in the slightest bit bored.' And then, looking round to make sure no-one could overhear, she said to him, 'It's been lovely dancing with Ryan, and getting to know him better. Have you enjoyed watching us dance?'

'Please, Sarah ...'

'I've seen you,' she said, her eyes sparkling with mischief. 'I've seen you watching us with that look on your face. You've enjoyed it even more than I have, and I've enjoyed it a lot. So keep watching, Charlie, I'm going to make it worth your while.'

Charles watched her go in a fever of dread and anticipation. The party had begun to thin out, and several of the men he'd talked to came over to make their farewells. He'd been glad of their company but he barely listened to them so taken up was he with watching Sarah. He saw Ryan go up to Alan and Rachel and thank them for the party. He was clearly about to leave, and Charles hoped he'd go without speaking to Sarah – his jealous anxiety had grown very strong again and he desperately wanted Sarah for his own – but then Sade's 'Your Love is King' began to play, and Sarah went over to Ryan and pulled him, laughing and pretending to resist, onto the dance-floor.

They lost themselves in the dance, surrendering to a slow, sensual rhythm that may as well have been sex. Ryan held Sarah close, his hands on her waist, and sometimes slipping a little lower. Swaying against him, Sarah laid her head on his chest, and seemed to give herself to him, body and soul.

Charles could only watch in fascinated horror and, when the song finally came to an end, he discovered that he was shaking and his hands were clenched so tightly his fingernails were digging painfully into his palms. Ryan and Sarah stayed in their embrace for long moments after the song had finished before separating and standing a few feet apart, unable to look at each other, or decide what to do next. In that moment Charles experienced a new terror. He was sure Sarah would go home with Ryan, go to his apartment and become his lover, but that terror instantly bred another even darker fear, and he saw himself driving his car while Sarah and Ryan kissed in the back seat, and then he saw Sarah and Ryan fucking in his bed at home while he stood by the bed, his head bowed in defeat. It was a soul-crushing yet deeply arousing image, and he shook his head to rid himself of it, but he looked up only to see Sarah coming towards him leading Ryan by the hand.

'Ryan's going now,' Sarah said, 'and he wants to say goodbye.'

'We must get together soon,' said Ryan, standing so close to Charles he loomed over him, 'and let bygones be bygones. Perhaps Sarah can arrange it as it looks likely we'll be meeting through work.'

Ryan held out his hand to Charles, offering him a handshake he had no intention of accepting, but Sarah spoke sternly to her husband.

'Oh, for heaven's sake, Charlie, don't be a spoilsport,' she said. 'Ryan's only being friendly.'

Overwhelmed, his face flushing with anger and shame, Charles took Ryan's hand, and had to suffer his rival's strong, manly grip.

'We'll meet again soon, I'm sure,' Ryan said with the same speck of derision in his eye Charles had first seen in Caroline Webster's eye all those years ago as a student at university. And then, turning from Charles as if he'd already forgotten him, he embraced Sarah, saying, 'It's been lovely to see you, Sarah, and get to know you better. I'll be in touch soon.'

'You bastard,' thought Charles, furious at Ryan's boldness but helpless against it.

'I look forward to it,' said Sarah, gazing up into Ryan's eyes. 'And thank-you for your company, Ryan, I've had a lovely evening.'

'I'm sorry it has to end,' said Ryan.

Charles noticed that Ryan's hand had moved from Sarah's waist round to her lower back where he placed it on the top curve of her bottom, and kept it there. Charles knew it for what it was, a demonstration of power, a gesture intended to let Charles know he'd laid claim to his wife, and been successful in his claim.

'I'm sorry too,' said Sarah, pressing against Ryan so eagerly one of his long legs pushed into the folds of her dress. 'Until the next time.'

'Until then,' said Ryan, kissing her lightly on her lips.

And then he was gone, walking quickly from the room.

Bereft by his departure, Sarah gave a sigh and looked at her stricken husband.

'Poor Charles,' she said gently. 'You look as if you've seen your own ghost.'

ON THEIR drive home Charles complained about the party, calling it a nightmare, and expressing his anger at Sarah for leaving him on his own for most of the evening, but Sarah just stretched sleepily in the passenger seat, and said, 'Nonsense, it wasn't a nightmare at all, more like a dream come true, you're just too scared to admit it.'

When he continued his complaints, and began to question her about her work connection with Ryan, and what he'd meant by 'I'll be in touch soon,' Sarah became impatient, and pulled rank on him.

'I've heard quite enough,' she said sharply. 'I don't want to hear another word, I mean it. What Ryan and I do is none of your business. You need to remember you're a slave, and don't have the right to question your Mistress. Now, leave me in peace,' she said, laying her head back and closing her eyes. 'Let me remember my lovely evening. I had a wonderful time, I don't want to forget a single moment.'

Quelled by her imperious manner, Charles drove in silence, but he was unable to stop himself from stealing glances at Sarah's lovely nylon-clad legs. Her dress had ridden up her thighs allowing him to glimpse the darker nylon at the tops of her stay-up stockings, and her legs were slightly apart, with one of her hands playing under the hem of her dress, touching herself through her panties, he was sure.

He knew she was thinking of Ryan, and the knowledge burned in him like fire even as it inflamed his submissive arousal. And the fact that she felt able to touch herself so intimately in front of him, as if he was of such little importance she could behave as she liked in his presence, shamed him terribly, and enslaved him all the more.

At this late hour the traffic in the city was light, and the journey took less than twenty minutes. When they got inside Sarah was so sleepy Charles had to help her upstairs, but she revived once they reached the bedroom.

'Take your clothes off,' she told him, her voice slurring slightly as she unfastened her string of pearls and dropped them on her dressing-table before kicking off her shoes. 'But keep your panties on. I like to see you in panties.'

She watched him as he undressed, saying, 'My prettiest pink panties, I'd forgotten you were wearing those. Maybe if I'd remembered I'd have told Ryan what you were wearing under your trousers. I have a feeling he'd like to have known, and I think you'd like me to have told him. You would have, wouldn't you?'

'No,' he protested weakly, his blood turning to water.

'Oh, I think you would,' she said, reaching behind her to unzip her dress. 'Never mind, I'll tell him next time we meet. "Charlie's wearing my panties," I'll tell him. "These days he wears them all the time. He's my slave now, and not a proper man. He wears a uniform too. Why don't you come round for a drink one night and I'll let you see Charlie in his uniform. It's quite a sight, I promise, and I'm sure he'll like you to see him in his uniform. He curtsies so nicely."'

Seeing the terror in his eyes, Sarah just laughed, and said, 'You mustn't be shy, Charlie. You look so sweet in my panties, and how hard they make you.'

Keeping her dress on, she tugged down her black silk knickers, and dangled then tauntingly from one of her fingers.

'You'll be wearing these tomorrow. What a lucky slave you are. And when you wear them I want you to remember these are the panties I was wearing when I was dancing with Ryan. These are the panties your Mistress was wearing when she was in the arms of another man.'

Dropping her knickers by her shoes, she went to her slave and stroked the tip of his erection where it protruded beyond his panties, saying with a new urgency, 'Tonight was so fucking sexy I thought I'd die of it, and you felt the same, didn't you? Answer me, Charlie.'

'Y-yes,' he stammered, longing for her.

'That's good,' she said, pushing him down on the bed and sitting astride him. He gazed up at her in wonder as she took down the front of her dress and removed her lace bra, freeing her lovely breasts. He could feel her stockings against his thighs, and the little net petticoat sewn into the lining of her dress scratched delightfully against his skin, and then, heaven of heavens, her warm wet, cunt pressed down on his erection, causing him to groan with desire, but she didn't take him inside. Instead, she moved tormentingly up and down his length, shivering with pleasure, and speaking in a husky whisper.

'Tonight was like one of my stories,' she said, 'but better, much better, because it wasn't a story, it was real.'

Leaning forward, she let her hair fall down around his face, and she too groaned in pleasure as his cock pulsed against her imperious cunt.

'When I saw you in your apron serving food, I thought I was dreaming,' she whispered in his ear. 'You looked so small and lost ... And to walk past you with Ryan at my side ... It was perfect ... And then to dance with Ryan knowing you were watching ... I wanted to kiss him, you know ... Kiss him and take him upstairs the way I do in my stories ... Oh, God, that's what I wanted ...'

Grinding against him, she lifted her head in ecstacy, and Charles took one of her breasts in his mouth, his tongue swirling around her hard nipple.

'You like that, don't you?' she said, taking her breast from him, and tormenting him with her other breast, touching it against his lips only to withdraw it again. 'Thinking of me with Ryan ... Thinking of me fucking him ... Tell me you like it,' she said, her breast the reward for his answer.

'I l-like it,' he stammered.

'You don't just like it,' she said, 'you love it.'

'Yes,' he gasped.

'Then say it.'

'I love it.'

Very aroused by his confession, she gave him her breast, thrilled by his need for it.

'There, now,' she said softly, 'that's for you.'

Lost in her beauty, Charles thrust up as he suckled, desperate to possess her, but she held herself just out of reach before pressing down on him again, once more sliding slowly, maddeningly up and down his length.

'I think Ryan knows,' she whispered. 'I don't know how he knows, but he does, I'm sure of it. I didn't tell him, I didn't say anything to give away our secret, but I think he knows all the same … That I'm your Mistress and you're my slave.'

Taking just the tip of his erection inside her, she held him there, a prisoner at the gates of heaven, and moved her breasts slowly from side to side, brushing her nipples against his lips.

'I felt it when you served us food,' she said. 'The way he looked at you with that smile in his eyes, and the way he called you Charlie … I could tell he knew … That you were my slave and I wanted him to take charge of you … And when we danced he knew you were watching, and he knew I knew too … And it excited him, I could feel his hardness through my dress … Oh God, his hardness … I came, Charlie, I did … Just from dancing with him … And he knew I came … I thought I'd faint from it but he held me until it passed … Good girl, he whispered in my ear … Good girl … He knows, Charlie, he knows you're my slave, and he knows I want to fuck him … And you want it too … You want him to fuck me …'

He cried out in pain, and bucked beneath her in a frenzy of arousal, but she was merciless.

'Tell me, Charlie,' she gasped, holding him down, 'Tell me you want me to fuck him.'

'I want you to fuck him,' he said, utterly enslaved by his wife and his rival.

'Then I will,' she sighed, taking him at last deep inside her, and moving with an urgent, violent rhythm. 'I'm going to fuck him … Fuck him and fuck him until I die of it.'

She felt him lose control, and she quickly followed, crying out in delight as the orgasm tore through them, leaving them limp and barely conscious. Stunned by pleasure, they lay in each other's arms, convinced they'd scaled the highest peak of sexual joy.

But they were wrong.

They were only in the foothills.

RYAN CALLED the office on Monday morning. He spoke to Alan Rennie, not Sarah, but he asked for Sarah to be present at the meeting he arranged for 11 o'clock on Wednesday morning in Alan's office. Alan was delighted with Sarah. She'd clearly worked her charms on Ryan, and if Joseph & Hill became a client it would be their fourth major new client since Sarah's Brexit Report had been circulated. Not only that, all their existing clients had renewed their contracts. She had become a major asset to the company.

Sarah teased and tormented Charles about her meeting with Ryan all through Monday and Tuesday evenings, telling him to look out her smartest clothes and prettiest underwear for Wednesday's meeting. As he served her in his black maid's dress and matching bobbed wig, she said, 'It'll be lovely to see him again. I wonder if he'll remember dancing with me. Perhaps he won't. He's such a handsome and charming man he'll have hundreds of women throwing themselves at him. All the same, I want to look my best, and you'll help me, won't you, Charlie?'

'Yes, Mistress,' Charles said, curtseying neatly in the way she'd taught him.

But on Tuesday evening Sarah took another opportunity to torment her slave. Her close friend Louise had called and asked to come round. Around six months ago she'd given up her job as a senior nurse in Accident and Emergency and opened a café with her business partner Miriam, also an ex-nurse, but Miriam's son had been badly hurt in a car accident in Australia, and she'd flown to Melbourne to help him recover. Without Miriam, Louise was struggling to keep the café open, and she wanted Sarah's help and advice.

Sarah knew Miriam was coming, but she hadn't told Charles who was tidying up after her meal in his maid's dress and wig, and she laughed aloud at the way he jumped with fright at the sound of the doorbell.

'I wonder who that can be,' she said to add to his torment. 'Perhaps you should go and see.'

He looked at her in terror, his hands wringing his apron, and she gave him a hug, saying, 'Don't worry, Charlie, you're not ready for that, but you'd better not go into the hall in case you're seen. Go into the scullery instead,' she said, pushing him into the little room off the kitchen, 'but don't make a sound or I'll have to introduce you to our guest.'

Charles trembled as he hid in the scullery and listened as Sarah answered the door and led her guest down the hallway, and into the kitchen. He recognised Louise's voice, and he could hear what they were saying so clearly he realised he mustn't make the slightest sound or Louise would hear him. She was an attractive, forceful woman, and he'd always tried to impress her, and the thought of her seeing him in his maid's uniform made him want to die. He looked down and saw his pretty white apron and the hem of his petticoat peeping out from under his dress, and his sheer hose and neat court shoes. 'What a fool I am,' he thought, trembling all the more, 'a stupid bloody fool.'

Louise told Sarah about her staffing problems at her café. 'I don't know how long Miriam will be in Australia. She thinks it will certainly be six weeks, maybe much longer. With her gone, I'm run off my feet. Most of my staff are mums who can work from 9.30 to 2.30 when their kids are at school but I'm really struggling with the breakfast shift from 7 till 9, and with Saturdays. Honestly, Sarah, I'm at my wit's end.'

'I'm sure we can think of something,' Sarah replied.

'If I have another week like this I'll have to close.'

'Nonsense,' said Sarah. 'Let me get this right – your real problem's with the early morning shifts and Saturdays?'

'Yes,' Louise said. 'If I can get reliable cover for those times I can stay open until Miriam gets back.'

'Then your problems are over,' said Sarah, amused to think of Charles listening from the scullery.

'What do you mean?' said Louise.

'Charles will cover for Miriam.'

'Charles?' Louise said in astonishment. 'Oh no, that's not possible.'

'Why not?'

'It's just not,' said Louise. 'He's so posh and important, I can't see him in a pinny cooking sausages and serving tables.'

'You don't know him the way I do,' said Sarah. 'He can roll his sleeves up when he wants to, and he's not above doing a hard day's work.'

'I still can't see it,' said Louise.

'Take my word for it,' said Sarah. 'Charles will be there tomorrow morning first thing, and he'll work for you until Miriam's son's fully recovered.'

'Shouldn't I ask him first?'

'I'll talk to him, don't worry, and he'll be there tomorrow, I promise, washed and shaved and raring to go.'

'He'll be paid, of course,' said Louise. 'It's not much, but I'll give him our highest rate.'

'That's alright,' said Sarah. 'He doesn't need to be paid.'

'I can't ask him to work for nothing.'

'No, but I can. He knows you're my friend and he'll be only too glad to help. Besides, he's not working at the moment, and he's got plenty of time on his hands. Consider it a favour between friends.'

'You're an angel,' said Louise. 'I don't know how to thank you.'

Charles raged in his prison. Serving Sarah was one thing, but serving one of her friends quite another. How dare she treat him like this, as her chattel? How dare she give him to another woman as if he was of no importance? And yet, even as he raged, he felt himself come erect.

'What can I do?' he thought in terror. 'How can I stand against her when every new indignity thrills me to the core?'

Helplessness engulfed him and, when Louise had left and Sarah came smiling into his prison, he could do nothing except fall to his knees before her.

'I thought so,' she said in satisfaction. 'I knew you'd like being given to another woman, and you'll do it, won't you, you'll work for Louise just as hard as you work for me?'

'Yes, Mistress,' he said, thrilled by his new slavery.

'Kiss my shoe.'

Immediately he bowed his head and planted adoring kisses on her elegant little shoe.

'How helpless you've become,' she said. 'I don't think there's anything now you wouldn't do for me.'

A tremor passed through him and his kisses became more frenzied.

'It's only a twenty minute walk to the café,' Sarah said, looking down with contempt on her befrocked husband. 'You'll leave the house at 6.30 and be there in plenty of time to start work at 7. You'll wear your manservant clothes – black trousers, a clean white shirt and smart black shoes, but you'll be wearing my panties underneath to remind you of your place. If I hear the slightest complaint from Louise about your work or attitude I'll tell her about our little secret, and about our new life. Is that understood?'

'Y-yes, Mistress,' he said, so lost in submission to her a part of him wanted her to tell Louise.

'Then you'd better get going, we both have busy days tomorrow. I want you to iron my red silk blouse and lay it out for the morning along with my Jaeger skirt and new shoes. And I'll want my prettiest underwear with a new pack of stay-up stockings. I'm sure you want me to look my best for my meeting with Ryan.'

'Yes, Mistress,' he said, his heart missing a beat.

'And you can set my place for breakfast, you won't have time in the morning.'

She turned away from him before he could reply, and busied herself on her lap-top preparing for her meeting while Charles carried out her instructions in a frenzy of anxious arousal.

Sarah made herself concentrate on work. The prospect of meeting Ryan again excited her greatly, but she knew he'd expect the highest professional standards from her, just as she did from herself, and she was determined to win Joseph & Hill as a client. Winning Ryan as her lover was a delicious thought but, for now at least, it couldn't get in the way of work.

It wasn't even 10 o'clock when she instructed Charles to run her bath, insisting he undress her and gather up her clothes before sending him off to bed. She knew how much waiting for her would excite him, and true enough, he was shivering with arousal when she came through after her bath. She was tired, and hurried him to orgasm with panty-sex and a crude story about her fucking Ryan while Charles waited by the bed in his maid's dress. When she woke refreshed in the morning it was well after 7, and Charles was already long gone.

AS SARAH had anticipated, the meeting with Ryan was difficult. He'd brought along Adam Bailey, the head of accounts at Joseph & Hill, and Ryan made it clear he had every confidence in Adam and his team, and was only considering consulting ACM over Brexit, and the possibly disastrous consequences of not being prepared for every outcome. Sarah, as the accountant with responsibility for overseas trade, would take the lead in the consultancy, and meet with Adam once a month, and provide him with regular, updated reports about likely trade and tariff options.

Sarah spoke confidently about the methods she'd use to underpin her advice, and she was very persuasive about the benefits of a bespoke Brexit consultancy. Both Ryan and Adam asked her some very challenging questions which she answered clearly and honestly, acknowledging the many difficulties she'd face. Her interrogators, while giving no indication they'd hire her, seemed satisfied with her answers.

'There's one last thing,' said Ryan after an hour of discussion. 'If Sarah's your lead on this I'll expect her to be a senior member of your staff. Certainly Adam will want to work with her on an equal footing, and it's clear the excellent Brexit Report was both Sarah's idea and her work. I take it that won't be a problem?'

'Actually, that's something we've been considering for some time,' Alan replied, not looking at Sarah. 'It won't be a problem.'

'In that case, I'll give you my answer this afternoon,' said Ryan, rising from his chair, shaking Sarah and Alan by the hand, and leaving the room with Adam.

'He's a hard bastard,' Alan said once Ryan was safely gone.

'He's good at his job, that's all,' said Sarah who'd been impressed with Ryan's tough-mindedness.

'Well, let's hope he bites,' said Alan. 'And as for your position here, let me make a few calls, and I'll get back to you as soon as I can.'

Sarah went for a walk to clear her head. Her meeting with Ryan had been entirely professional, and yet she hadn't failed to notice how good he looked in his dark suit and white shirt and, now the meeting was over, she allowed herself to recall how much she'd enjoyed dancing and talking with him at the party. And she couldn't help but be grateful for his suggestion she be made more senior at ACM, and she wondered what offer Alan would make her, if any. At that moment her phone received a text. She was surprised to see it was from Ryan, and then she remembered her mobile number was on the business card she'd given him. She opened the text and read – 'I've called Alan and told him I have another option – to poach you at double your salary. Good luck.'

Sarah flushed with excitement. She knew Ryan didn't need her at Joseph & Hill, and had only called Alan to improve her bargaining power with ACM. But double her salary? She couldn't expect Alan to go that high. It was out of the question, she told herself, it had to be.

Alan called her into his office at 3 o'clock.

'Good news, Sarah,' he said, smiling benignly. 'I've spoken with the chairman and the other partners and we've agreed to make you a senior accountant.'

'Thank-you, Alan,' she replied. 'At what salary?'

He named a figure. It was a large increase on her current salary and, under normal circumstances, she'd have jumped at it, but Ryan had made her think more highly of her worth.

'That's less than I was hoping for,' she said, keeping her manner firm and a little cold.

'Really?' said Alan, surprised by her reply. 'I thought we were being very generous. What figure did you have in mind?'

She named her price. It wasn't quite what Ryan had suggested, but it wasn't far off.

'That's preposterous,' Alan said, turning pale.

'You may say so,' Sarah said, holding her nerve, 'but I should tell you I've received an even higher offer, so you can hardly blame me if I ask for slightly less, out of a sense of loyalty, of course.'

'Of course,' said Alan, very flustered. 'I'm afraid I'll have to make a few more calls, if you'll bear with me.'

He called him into his office again an hour later and gave her the news that her terms had been accepted. Hiding her astonishment, she listened while he told her that not only would she be receiving the salary she'd requested, but she would be given a larger office and her own personal assistant. And she would now also be entitled to her own reserved parking space in the basement car park, but she didn't like driving in the city, and wouldn't need it.

'There's some other news,' said Alan who didn't seem at all happy to have agreed Sarah's terms. 'Ryan Moore has just called. He's taking you on as their Brexit consultant on a six-month renewable contract.'

'That's wonderful,' said Sarah, her cup running over.

'It is,' said Alan, 'but with power comes expectation, and don't forget it. You'll earn every last penny of your salary, I can promise you that.'

Sarah knew he was right, but she didn't let his mean-spirited comment dampen her spirits. Why should she? They wouldn't be paying her so much unless she was worth it, and she backed herself to rise to the challenge.

When she arrived home she was still too wrapped up in the events of her day to pay much attention to her neatly uniformed maid.

'Bring me a glass of wine in the living-room,' she instructed him as he hung up her coat. When he brought her the wine, she simply said, 'That will be all for now, thank-you, Charlie. I'll call you if I need anything.' She didn't even notice him curtsey before he left the room.

She took out her phone, and looked through her messages, reading again the text from Ryan. She wanted to thank him, but didn't want to go beyond professional limits, so she kept it simple and texted – 'Such good news. I'm very much looking forward to working for Joseph & Hill.'

A few minutes later she received a reply which she read eagerly.

'Good news indeed, but I wonder if I may ask something of you. Would it be alright if I called you?'

She stared at the screen, her heart pounding and her face flushed with excitement, and then she texted in reply –

'Yes of course.'

Before she could gather herself, her phone rang and she answered it.

'I hope you don't mind me calling,' Ryan said.

'Not at all,' she said.

'Thank-you,' he said, and then he fell silent.

'Ryan?' she said. 'Are you still there?'

'I'm still here,' he said, and then he went silent again before saying, 'Look, Sarah, I don't know how to say this so I'm just going to say it, alright?'

'Yes,' she said, her excitement mounting.

'I've been wanting to call you for days, ever since the party, but I didn't have your number, and then there was the meeting today. I thought it would be best to wait until that was over because this isn't … this isn't to do with work?'

'Isn't it?' she said, suddenly feeling as foolish as a teenage girl.

'No, it isn't,' he said. 'I very much enjoyed our time at Alan's party, and then meeting you today … Well, I'd like to see you again.'

'See me?' she said, her head a mess.

'Yes,' he said.

'On my own?'

'Yes.'

'Not with Charles?' she said by instinct.

'No, not with Charles,' he said. 'I think it's best we get to know each other a little better before bringing Charles into things.'

'And it's not about work?' she said, deeply aroused by his strange comment about Charles. Did he really know Charles was her slave? Had he read her mind? Did he know how much it thrilled her to think of fucking him in front of Charles? Like her, did Ryan want to flaunt their passion in front of her helpless slave? Did he want to fuck her while Charles knelt by the bed in his little maid's uniform? Did he want to discipline Charles while she watched in joy and wonder at his mastery over her husband?

Of course he knew, and of course that's what he wanted, Sarah understood with a thrill of excitement. Why else had she felt such a connection with him at Alan's party? Why else had she come in his arms while they were dancing in front of Charles? They were soul-mates, fellow dominants, partners in crime.

'It's definitely not about work,' Ryan said. 'I hope that's alright.'

'I don't see why not,' she said, amazed her voice held steady. 'Do you have somewhere in mind?'

'Actually, I don't,' he said, laughing and sounding sweetly nervous. 'I haven't thought that far ahead.'

Tonight, she thought. Right now, anywhere, the street, a bar, just say and I'll be there.

'An evening would be best, but everything's so hectic. I'm free Saturday midday. Could we have lunch?'

'I'd like that,' she said, hiding her disappointment. How could she wait two whole days?

'If you come to my apartment, I'll cook something for you.'

'Sounds good,' she said, coming round to the idea.

'I'll try not to poison you.'

You already have, she thought.

'What time?' she said.

'Around 12.30. I'll text you my address.'

'Fine, I'll be there.'

'That's great,' he said.

'I'll look forward to it.'

'Me too.'

'Until Saturday, then.'

'Until Saturday,' he said, and then he ended the call.

Sarah sat in a daze trying to come to terms with what had just happened. She was going to be alone with Ryan Moore. The thought both frightened and aroused her. Flirting with him at a party could be dismissed as the folly of an evening, and making up stories about him for Charles could be seen as no more than a fantasy shared between husband and wife, but agreeing to meet Ryan at his apartment was of a different order. This was real and this was dangerous. This was playing with fire, and this, more than anything, was what she wanted, if only she had the courage to see it through.

For a moment she lost her nerve, fearful of hurting Charles too grievously and of losing the safe haven of her marriage, and she determined not to meet Ryan on Saturday, but she knew she was kidding herself. Of course, she would go. Nothing in the world could stop her. Her enslavement of Charles, the way her stories had developed to include her taking a lover, and the powerful sensual connection she'd felt with Ryan at Alan's party all conspired to make her date with Ryan inevitable. And as for Charles, well he'd just have to cope as best he could. He was her slave, after all – wasn't he at that moment waiting for her in the kitchen in his maid's dress and apron? – and she knew how much it thrilled him to submit to her, and suffer for her pleasure.

At that moment her phone rang again, and she answered it quickly, thinking it might be Ryan, but it wasn't, it was Louise.

'Just wanted to give you a report on Charles,' she said.

'Charles?' Sarah said, lost for a moment. 'Oh, yes, of course. I've just got in and my head's all over the place.'

My God – you send your husband to slave for another woman and then forget all about it!

'How did he do?' Sarah asked quickly, hoping to cover up her forgetfulness.

'What can I say?' said Louise, 'except that he's a bloody marvel. Honestly, Sarah, he was brilliant, and so quick and good-natured about everything. I'd never have believed it of him, but nothing was too much trouble – the angry customers rushing for their trains, the till, cooking, waiting table, washing-up – he even fixed the dodgy handle on the fridge.'

'I told you,' said Sarah, happy that Charles had done so well, and moved by his endeavours. She knew that by serving Louise he was really serving her.

'Well, you were right,' said Louise. 'I told him he could go at 9, but he stayed until 10, and the kitchen was spotless when he left.'

'I should think so too,' said Sarah.

'Tell me I'm not dreaming,' said Louise. 'Tell me I can have him till Miriam gets back.'

'He's all yours.'

'Be careful,' said Louise. 'If Miriam sees what he's like, she'll want to keep him.'

'I'm sure that could be arranged.'

'Well, give him a big kiss from me, he's earned it.'

'I will,' Sarah said.

She didn't kiss her busy little maid, but she put her arms around him, and gave him a big hug instead.

'Forgive me, Charlie,' she said. 'I've had such a day I forgot all about you working for Louise, but I've just had a lovely call from her. She's delighted with your work this morning, and so am I. I want you to work like that every day until Miriam gets back from Australia. Maybe longer. It rather amuses me to have you working in a café. You'll do that for me, won't you?'

'Yes, Mistress,' he said in a voice so small and meek it held barely a trace of the man she'd married. Charles Hunter was getting smaller and smaller, and further and further away and, if she wasn't careful, he'd vanish altogether.

'I'm very pleased with you,' she said, darkly aroused by the helplessly servile creature she'd created. 'I think you deserve a reward, in fact I'm sure you do. Tell me, what would you like?'

He looked at her nervously, fearful she was teasing him.

'Don't be shy, Charlie, tell me what you'd like.'

'A k-kiss,' he stammered.

'A kiss?' she said. 'What kind of kiss? A little kiss on the cheek?'

'No,' he said, hardly looking at her.

'What, then? A proper kiss? A real husband and wife kiss?'

'Y-yes,' he said, a tremor in his voice.

'That's sweet of you, Charlie, really it is,' she said, 'but I think the time for that is over. Only real men get kisses like that, not silly kitchen-maids.'

A shiver passed through him, and tears misted his eyes, and Sarah thought he was the sweetest maid she'd ever seen, and yet she wondered at herself, and at how far things had gone. This was too much, of course it was, but she couldn't help herself. She'd wanted to be kind, she really had, but it was much more fun to be cruel and, seeing him so meek and cowed only made her want to hurt him all the more.

'How about this for your reward?' she said. 'After I've enjoyed the meal you've cooked for me, you can come through to the living-room and kneel at my feet the way you like. You can give my feet a rub. If you're very good I'll let you kiss them, I know how much you like that too, and I'll tell you all my news from the day. It's been a wonderful day, and there's so much I want to tell you. How about that, Charlie? Does that sound good?'

'Yes, Mistress,' he said, wiping his eyes.

'Then that's what we'll do,' she said.

KNEELING BEFORE Sarah, Charles was overwhelmed by conflicting emotions. He hadn't lost his pride, but it had become long submerged beneath his submissive yearnings. Even as he massaged Sarah's nylon-clad foot, pride still burned in his heart and mind, but the flames only fuelled his masochistic joy by reminding him of all he had lost, and when he looked at Sarah's pretty foot resting on his apron and, beneath that, the lacy hem of his slip peeping out from under his maid's dress, he hated how foolish he must look, and yet he loved to feel so shamed and helpless in front of the woman he loved.

None of it made sense. How could he be in heaven and hell at the same time? But then he'd given up trying to make sense of it. He'd sunk down too deep in the quicksand, and struggling would only hasten his doom.

Charles heard Sarah's sigh of pleasure as he rubbed his thumbs over the warm slippery nylon sheathing her sole, and his heart lifted at the sound of her contentment. More than anything he loved to please her, but then perhaps he loved to please all women for, greatly to his surprise, he'd enjoyed his morning working for Louise.

She'd been easy to work for, he recalled. She led by example, never stopping work in the three hours he'd been there. She gave clear instructions without becoming rude or impatient, and her machine made excellent coffee, and the food was of the highest quality so that it was a pleasure to serve her many customers. He knew he'd been an able assistant, and he wasn't surprised to hear that Louise had told Sarah she'd been delighted with his work. But there was the truth of it. The knowledge that he'd pleased Sarah by pleasing her friend was the real source of his strange new pride, the pride a slave takes in pleasing his Mistress.

'That feels heavenly,' Sarah murmured sleepily when Charles started work on her other foot. 'And my meal was delicious too. I'm so full and comfy, I could stay here forever. It hardly seems fair, does it, Charlie? I make you into my slave and, instead of punishing me for being cruel and selfish, the world has decided to smile on me. I've had such a lovely day,' she said, stretching lazily. 'Would you like me to tell you about it?'

'Yes, Mistress,' he said, thrilled by her spoiled manner, and by the prospect of hearing of her success while he worshipped on his knees.

'The meeting with Ryan was difficult. He asked very tough questions and I had to really be on my toes, but he seemed to like my answers. Adam

Bailey was there too, their Head of Accounts. I formed a good impression of him. He worked for you when you were CEO, didn't he?'

'Yes,' he said, finding it painful to remember his previous status.

'Was he good at his job?'

'He was excellent.'

'I'm pleased to hear it, for I'll be working most closely with him.'

'So they t-took you on?'

'Oh, yes, didn't I say? I'm now Brexit consultant to Joseph & Hill, and four other new companies as well, and that's on top of my existing clients. But that's not all, Charlie. Ryan made it clear he wouldn't expect to deal with anyone other than a Senior Accountant, and Alan had no choice but to promote me, and at nearly double my salary. You should have seen his face, he went as white as a sheet. So now do you see how the world has smiled on me today? I'm so lucky, I can hardly take it in. Are you happy for me, Charlie?'

'Yes, Mistress,' he said, crushed by her success. It left him feeling even more outdone and left behind.

'But don't forget what a help you've been,' she said. 'Helping me with my report – that's what's done the trick, you know – and becoming by devoted little housemaid, and looking after me so well. I feel so loved and supported, you've no idea, and so free and strong. I love living like this, Charlie, really I do,' she said, leaning forward, and taking his head gently in her hands. 'But there's something else I have to tell you. It will be very hard for you to hear, and will hurt you very much, so I want you to be brave. Can you do that, Charlie? Can you be brave for me, very brave?'

'I'll t-try,' he said in a trembling voice.

'I'm sure you will,' she said, both moved and irritated by his meekness, 'but trying's not enough, I'm afraid, you need to really be brave. I'm going to ask a lot of you, and set you a very hard test. Are you ready for that test?'

'Yes,' he said, wanting to be brave for his Mistress.

'Do you promise?'

'Yes, Mistress,' he said, hoping he could keep his word.

'Kiss my knees,' she said, opening her legs a little. 'Go on, kiss my knees, and look up my skirt if you like. It will sugar the pill.'

Trembling with excitement, he pressed his mouth to her shapely knees, and gazed under her skirt at the long valley of her thighs, and the distant white heaven of her panties. Sarah was right, it did sugar the pill. Tormented yet enthralled by the lovely sight, he felt better able to be brave, and to submit to her will.

'I had another call tonight,' she told him. 'It was from Ryan.'

Pain shot through Charles even as arousal flashed in his blood, and he pressed his mouth harder against Sarah's knees.

'He wants to see me again,' she said, 'and I've agreed to see him. It's not about work this time. It's not business, Charlie, it's pleasure.'

Charles groaned in agony, and hid his head between Sarah's knees, pushing her legs further apart.

'This Saturday, Charlie, I'm going on a date with Ryan Moore. I'm going to his apartment at lunch-time. We'll be alone together all day. You'll be working in Louise's café and I'll be alone with Ryan. It's not a story,' she told him, her own arousal growing urgent. 'It's real this time, real and true, and I want you to accept it. I know it will hurt, but I want you to suffer it for me as my slave. Will you do that for me, Charlie?'

'Yes,' he called out in an ecstasy of pain. 'Yes, yes.'

'You'll take this from me?'

'Yes.'

'And you'll still love me?'

'Yes.'

'I knew you would,' she gasped. 'My stories have prepared us for this, shown us the way, and you want it as much as me, I know you do. Tell me you want it.'

'I want it,' he cried out, his heart breaking into pieces even as his cock came fully erect.

'Then here,' Sarah said, tugging up her skirt and taking down her panties. 'This is for you, all for you.'

His hunger endless, he fed on her lovely, faithless cunt.

THE TWO days before Sarah's date with Ryan passed more easily for Sarah than Charles. Sarah was exceptionally busy at work, moving in to her new office, and striving to keep up with the demands of her new and existing clients. She pushed hard to be given the new intern Helen Gould as her assistant, and was delighted when she succeeded. Helen was young and bright, and well able to work on her own initiative. Sarah knew that some of the other accountants, envious of her salary, were hoping she'd wither under her new responsibilities, but she felt confident she'd succeed. She didn't carry her domestic dominance into work, but something of it rubbed off on her, and she felt entirely at ease in her promoted role.

It was harder for Charles. His mornings at the café gave him some respite – the work was so hectic and full-on he didn't have time to think about Sarah and Ryan, but as soon as he got home he became consumed by fear and a head-spinning anxiety that stayed with him all through the day and night.

He couldn't let it happen. He couldn't just stand by and let Sarah have an affair with his worst enemy, and yet he felt helpless to stop her. Not only did he feel a deep and shameful arousal at the thought of being cuckolded by Ryan, but he'd become so subordinate to Sarah, and so addicted to the pleasure he found in submission, he could barely imagine speaking to her, let alone challenging her authority.

But on Friday evening, the eve of Sarah's date with Ryan, Charles gathered the courage to speak his mind.

She was working in her study and Charles, in his black maid's uniform and neat bobbed wig, knocked on the door, something Sarah now insisted on as a matter of course. 'It keeps things right,' she'd said.

'Come in,' she replied, sounding impatient.

'Mistress?' he said quietly when he came into the room.

He hadn't curtsied as he thought that might weaken his case, but she was too busy on her computer to notice his omission.

'What is it?' she said briskly, not looking up from the screen.

'Can I talk to you?'

'If you're quick.'

'I w-want to talk about … about…' he stammered, intimidated by her manner.

'Get on with it.'

'I want to talk about t-tomorrow.'

'Do you indeed?' she said, smiling as she looked up at him. 'You want to talk about my date with Ryan?'

'Y-yes.'

'I wondered if you'd get round to that,' she said, leaning back in her chair. 'Well, what do you want to say about it?'

'I love you,' he blurted, suddenly overcome with emotion. 'You're my wife, and I love you and don't want to lose you.'

And then, greatly to his shame, he burst into tears.

Sarah got quickly to her feet and went to him, putting her arms around him and rubbing his back.

'I know you love me, you silly thing,' she said, 'and I love you too, maybe not in the way I used to, but it's love all the same, I promise. How could a Mistress not love such a sweet and adorable slave?'

'Please, Sarah, don't go to him.'

'Oh, come on, now, we've been through all this.'

'Please,' he implored her, 'I couldn't bear to lose you.'

'You're not going to lose me,' she said, both moved and aroused by his tears. 'You'll still be my slave, and I'll still be your Mistress. You'll run my baths, and cook for me, wash my clothes and run errands for me. In many ways we'll be closer than ever, can't you see that?'

He took a deep, shuddering breath but it did no good. His tears just fell all the harder.

'Stop your tears,' Sarah said in a much firmer voice. 'They won't do any good. Look at you, in your little dress and apron with tears running down your face. You're not a man any more, and it's time you faced up to that once and for all. You're my slave now, my maid, and that's why I need a real man in my life. You understand that, I know you do, so dry your eyes, and learn to be true to yourself. The time for hiding has long passed. You want this, Charlie, and so do I.'

Chastened by her firm tone, Charles took long, deep breaths, and stopped his tears.

'That's more like it,' said Sarah, still rubbing his back. 'You made me a promise to be brave, and I expect you to keep your promise. You'll do that, won't you? You'll do it for your Mistress?'

Blinking back tears, all resistance gone, Charles nodded his head.

'There's my slave,' she said tenderly, 'my sweet and obedient housemaid. Now, come upstairs with me. I have something I need your help with.'

Sarah took him upstairs to their bedroom where she tried on a number of dresses for her date with Ryan, asking Charles' advice on which one suited her best. She also asked him to choose her lingerie, smiling warmly when he laid out her loveliest matching bra and panties in white silk, and a pair of her sheerest stay-up stockings.

'Thank-you, Charlie,' she said. 'Those are lovely.'

It was the middle of a warm July and Sarah settled on a light summery dress in a pretty red floral pattern with some high-heeled sandals.

'What do you think?' she asked Charles, walking up and down in her dress.

Charles gazed at her in wonder, moved by how young and beautiful she looked. The thin straps made the most of her lovely shoulders, and the loose flowing hem flipped and swayed beguilingly round her knees.

'It's just a simple little dress,' she said, frowning at her reflection in the mirror, 'but it's quite pretty, don't you think? And I don't want to look as if I'm trying too hard.'

'You look lovely,' Charles said, awed by her beauty, and deeply, darkly aroused by the knowledge that he was helping her look her best for another man.

'You're sweet,' she said, still looking at her reflection. 'And the pretty undies you've chosen for me will feel lovely under it, I'm sure. Yes, I'll wear this dress,' she declared, turning sideways to study her profile. 'I won't need a jacket, but I'll take my little silk cardigan in case a breeze gets up.'

Later, in bed, Sarah calmed him with panty-sex, telling him a torrid little tale about how she planned to invite Ryan to the house for a meal.

'Well, it's only fair,' she said, 'as he's invited me for lunch. And you'll cook for us, Charlie, something delicious in his honour. And you'll serve at table in your uniform and apron, your blue dress, I think, with your pretty blond wig. And you'll curtsey to him whenever he gives you an instruction,' she added so that he groaned in helpless arousal. 'And you won't call him Ryan. Oh, no, that won't do at all. You'll call him sir, or Mister Moore, I'll let him decide which.'

Charles groaned and shivered, and she knew his orgasm was close.

'It will be terribly embarrassing for you, Charlie,' she said, sweetly certain her tale would come true, 'of course it will, but you'll get used to it in time, you'll even grow to like it, and when you see us together you'll know, you'll know this is the way things have to be.'

Her words flicked a switch in his brain and, with a cry of loss and pain, Charles emptied himself into the soft bundle of Sarah's hose. When his breathing had slowed, Sarah put her arms around him, and held him close, whispering softly, 'It's going to happen, Charles, I promise. Try to be happy if you can. You've already given up everything for me, you may as well enjoy it.'

'I love you, Sarah,' he murmured as if from a dream.

'I should think you do,' she answered, smiling as she drifted into sleep.

Also by Molly Sands – Cruel Heaven, The Devlin Woman, A New Devotion, An Obedient Husband, Slave Song, Magda, Contessa, Sacred Days.

Printed in Great Britain
by Amazon

49305549R00097